MYRI'S HANDS

Jane Roop

S & H Publishing, Inc.
Purcellville, Virginia

Jane Roop/S & H Publishing, Inc.
P. O. Box 456
Purcellville, VA 20134
www.sandhpublishing.com

Publisher's Note: This is a work of fiction. Names, characters, places, and incidents are a product of the author's imagination. Locales and public names are sometimes used for atmospheric purposes. Any resemblance to actual people, living or dead, or to businesses, companies, events, institutions, or locales is completely coincidental.

Ordering Information:
Quantity sales. Special discounts are available on quantity purchases by corporations, associations, and others. For details, contact the "Special Sales Department" at the address above.

Myri's Hands/ Jane Roop. -- 1st ed.
ISBN 978-1-63320-026-5 Print Edition
ISBN 978-1-63320-027-2 Ebook Edition

At night in sleep I slip away, my other, she – wanders.
—ACROSS THE TIGHTWIRE
by Jane Roop

CHAPTER ONE

Figure It Out

Myri reached for the padlock. It slid across the glass counter top and slapped into her hand like a pitched baseball into a glove. She glanced up to see if anyone had noticed. Especially the customer, a young man in motorcycle leathers who'd placed the shiny padlock in front of the cash register, but he'd walked away in search of a cable. He left behind the mingled scent of oiled leather and cigarette smoke.

Her heart pounded. She needed this part-time job. After paying for her father's funeral, very little was left in her savings account.

"This is ridiculous," she mumbled and checked for a price tag. Ridiculous and potentially damaging. What if one of the customers told Sol?

Would Sol put up with a new employee who was a bit strange?

Earlier in the day, a Phillips screwdriver had rolled effortlessly across the counter into her outstretched hand. Mr. Hanlin, a retired accountant and a regular at Sol's Hardware, had watched the screwdriver's progress with squinty-eyed curiosity. Myri returned his inquisitive frown with a shrug and a smile. She'd held her breath as she handed him his change, terrified he would wander into the back as he often did for a chat with Sol Sheenski, the store's owner. Just remembering him turning on his heel and leaving the store gave Myri a feeling of relief. What could she say? She didn't have a clue what was going on or why. Lately, her hands had a power of their own and often throbbed with heat.

Other peculiarities in her life she'd learned to live with silently at an early age. In the beginning, she tried to explain. "Foolishness." Her dad had shaken his head and puckered his lips. He was a practical man, living a hard life, raising a daughter after his wife's early death. He didn't need or want her weirdness. Myri thought she detected a change in his view right at the end.

"You'll figure it out," he'd struggled to say from the hospital bed. "Trust yourself, but don't blab about it," and then he smiled a smile that transformed his face. As his blue eyes softened, his bulbous nose, red and veined from years of smoking and drinking, gave his face the merry look of a clown. *"Remember, trust yourself."* Those were the last words he'd spoken to her. She'd held his hand and let the tears run down her cheeks.

Perhaps he finally saw the unseen around him, felt the spirits. Perhaps he left the world comforted by a new understanding. Myri hoped so.

In contrast, Myri's world grew wackier and less comfortable. Now objects came flying into her hands on odd occasions for no reason or purpose that she could understand.

"Definitely a good thing I'm seeing Molly today."

"What?" The biker returned with the cable.

"Nothing, just talking to myself." Myri reached for the cable, relieved that it at least came passively from his hand to hers. She rang up his purchases, took his twenty and handed him the change. She watched him through the plate glass window in front as he walked outside to the Harley where he stowed the items in a saddlebag before adjusting his helmet and strapping it snug. After kicking up the stand, he straddled the bike with muscular ease and familiarity. He fired the engine, revved it. The blast of pipes rattled the window. He left the parking lot, taking a right into the curb lane. At the light, he had a free right turn. With a quick look left, he raced the engine, leaned forward and gunned the bike in an effort to beat an advancing green Subaru.

"Oh no." Myri clamped a hand over her mouth.

In slow motion the bike toppled in front of the Subaru, and then spun like a merry-go-round. The brakes on the Subaru screeched, but there was no avoiding the collision. The biker lay sprawled in the middle of the intersection.

A line of bold hyphenated bursts of energy arched over the biker's body, a sure sign that he was no longer alive. She knew what would come next; it was too late for anything else.

Once she'd tried to explain it to Mrs. Grossenbacker, her fourth grade teacher. It was simple enough. When energy bowed over a body like a rainbow without color or went around a body, that creature was no longer alive. It was no longer connected by vibrating strands to a world that shimmered like a jeweled net. Then a spirit came. Myri had been sent to the office with a note. "No wonder this child can't do long division. She lives in a fantasy world."

Her father crumpled the note the office sent home. He shook his head, and reached for a pack of cigarettes.

"Myri, zip it. I got enough trouble." He struck a match, cloistered the flame, dipped the tip of the cigarette towards it. "You and your mother. Damn spirits didn't do her much good, did they?" He whipped the match to and fro and then tossed it into an ashtray.

After that Myri zipped it. No more talking about energy fields, arches, and spirits—at least with humans. Dogs understood. In the past, whenever Myri really needed a confidante, she'd turned to Lucy, a chocolate Lab with adoring eyes and a head cocked with attention. But Lucy was long gone. No adoring, comforting dog waited at home.

Several customers raced from the shopping aisles to the front window to find out what had happened. They couldn't see the spirit. Today, like the day her father died, Ruby came. Plump, with fat brown cheeks and long silky black hair, she wore a red caftan that floated around her like a mist.

"I'll call 911," one customer shouted.

"Hey, Myri, what's happening up there?"

The voice from the back belonged to Sol Sheenski, the owner. His bald head bobbed up and down as he craned his neck over the displays on the counter that separated the general hardware from the inventory of small auto parts shelved in cubicles behind him.

Her throat ached. Her eyes stung. She stood rooted, unable to respond.

"Myri, what's the deal?" he yelled.

She heard the squeak of hinges as he raised the counter flap, followed by his hurried steps up the aisle. They stood side by side, a Mutt and Jeff picture: Myri, petite with a cap of black short, spiked hair, and Sol over six feet tall, thin and pale as pulled taffy.

The revolving wail of an ambulance grew louder.

Customers moved from inside the store to the sidewalk.

"Sol, there's nothing we can do." Her voice trembled. "I'm so sorry, but I have to leave. I have an appointment at eleven and I don't want to be late."

"Go on." Sol waved a dismissal. "Dana will be here any minute."

Myri grabbed her purse from under the counter and edged around Sol. She pulled a black down ski jacket from a hook beside the back door before stepping out into a sunny but cold February afternoon. The winter pansies, as well as the flowering purple kale at the edge of the building, drooped in the icy air.

The piercing wail of the ambulance stopped. She looked right, saw the ambulance roll by, and then turned to walk in the opposite direction.

Ten minutes from the store, she paused at the corner of Main and River and waited for the light to change so she could cross the busy thoroughfare. She sucked in a deep breath. A shudder ran through her as she replayed the scene of the motorcycle out of control. There was nothing the driver of the Subaru could have done to avoid the shattering impact, nothing could have stayed the sound of metal crunching on metal, and nothing could change the black figure in an immobile heap on the pavement. But at least there was Ruby to help with the transition.

Myri glanced at the crosswalk panels, heard the steady ticking of the time regulating the lights. She was impatient to be on her way, and then she saw Ruby on the other side of the street waving at her.

"Ruby, what are you doing here?" Myri called out.

"Crossing now allowed. Fifteen seconds, fourteen seconds," an automated voice coached pedestrians.

Myri, concentrating on Ruby, stepped off the curb before she looked to her left. A semi-truck barreled down the street. The cab, bright red, sparkled in the crystal air. Red, her dad's favorite color, she thought, then froze. Her feet were rooted to the pavement. In a desperate act of resignation, she closed her eyes and flung her hands up, palms out, as if to shield herself from the blow.

First she was repelled, slapped back with a force that knocked the breath out of her, and then she felt the wind as the truck passed. She lay flat on the sidewalk, staring into a blue, cloudless sky while the cold from the cement seeped through her coat.

Slowly she rolled to her side and then sat up. After several deep breaths, she still trembled. Nothing was broken, though there was no doubt she had a few sore spots. She wiped bits of gravel off her hands, swung her head around to see if anyone had seen what happened. No one was nearby. A pedestrian coming towards her was too far away.

Across the street Ruby, a huge grin on her face, shimmered in red light. She pushed her arm forward, her right hand clinched in a thumbs-up gesture of approval.

Myri swallowed hard and raised a right hand that now throbbed with heat, to return the salute. Both hands, in fact, were swollen and tingling, as if they had been walloped. She inspected them carefully. They'd saved her life, but how? Something propelled her out of the way of the huge truck.

Maybe Ruby could explain. Myri stood, hoping to make the crossing to Ruby's side. But now Ruby wasn't alone. Beside her stood Myri's father in a red and black plaid flannel shirt he'd loved, despite its frayed collar and cuffs. He hooked one arm around Ruby's waist and waved so-long with the other. The two of them faded away before the light flashed "walk" and the automated voice began.

"Hey, lady, it says walk." Myri turned to face a teenaged boy in tattered blue jeans with ragged holes in both knees. Greasy, unwashed hair fell long and limp around acne-scarred cheeks. A pair of ear buds dangled around his neck. "You going or what?"

"I'm not sure," she said. The boy shuffled around her.

She took the appointment card out of her pocket, frowned at its bold, gilded logo.

Molly Seward Psychic Healer By appointment only.

"Trust yourself," her dad had said. "You'll figure it out. Just don't blab about it."

She headed back to the store, wondering if she should call Molly or if Molly already knew she wasn't coming today.

Myri checked her cell. She'd missed two calls: one from Chris and one from Molly. Both had left messages.

"Myri, we really need some help tomorrow. Lena and Sam are both out with the flu. I know Sunday's your only day off and it's Valentine's Day, but I'm desperate."

Since she was saving for college tuition and was currently boyfriendless, a condition she often found herself in, she called Chris back and left a message that she would see him tomorrow.

Molly's message was more intriguing. "Thanks for letting me know you couldn't make it. We can re-schedule or just talk over the phone." There was a pause with no hang-up click, and then more message. "Actually, I think I should tell you to be very mindful at any intersections. Hope to hear from you soon."

Myri deleted both messages, but not without a pause of her own. If she ever really needed to blab, she knew Molly would be the right person.

CHAPTER TWO

Shorts and Sandals?

"Myri, thank God you could come," Chris said. A frigid north wind slipped in behind her.

"Where are your gloves?" Chris crossed the entry and shoved on the slow-closing, massive, oak entry door. "You'll end up sick too, if you aren't careful."

Myri pressed the back of her hand to Chris' cheek. "Plenty warm, huh?"

She uncurled a black scarf from around her neck.

"At least you have a coat, which is more than I can say for that lot." He pitched a thumb in the direction of the crowd huddled along the tasting room counter. "What a crazy day. As if a banquet and a wedding on the same day isn't enough, those guys showed up from nowhere. Just look at them in shorts and sandals. Not a coat in sight."

Chris shook his head in disgust. He was as he always was: clean-shaven and absolutely tidy in gray slacks, white shirt, a wine colored V-necked pullover sweater and tie. Today's tie was bright red with rows of white cupids in honor of the lovers' holiday.

"They're dressed like they're going to a luau. All they need is a ukulele," Myri said.

"You should've seen the tour guide. She was dressed in a red muumuu and half dozen leis around her neck. She went back to the van for something. It wouldn't surprise me if she comes back with a ukulele."

"Did they come in the white van in the lower lot, the one with the Desert Imp Tours logo? That's a new one I haven't heard of before."

"I don't know. Like I said, they didn't call ahead to make arrangements."

"They're going to freeze when they go outside," Myri said. The short walk from the employee's parking lot left everything – her ears, her nose, her toes; everything except her hands – aching from the cold.

"The way they're drinking, they won't even notice the cold."

It was true. Proof: like two dragonflies, Stella and Stephanie flitted back and forth behind the long counter, refilling empty glasses.

"Come on, the twins can take care of that crowd." He waved for Myri to follow him. "And the drinkers, don't worry about them." He jerked along, pumping both arms as if in a race walking contest, a cell phone in one hand and a clipboard in the other. "They have a driver. They'll be safe."

"So where do you want me? Out front?" Myri asked.

Once inside the employee common area – a putty-colored room with four tables in the center – she slipped off her coat. A row of gray metal lockers along one wall faced two vending machines and a water cooler. Next to the water cooler sat a dusty dieffenbachia in a knee-high green plastic planter. Myri followed Chris to a chrome and yellow Formica-topped table.

"No," he said. He thumbed through a couple of pages on the clipboard. After a quick glance at his cell phone, he rubbed his chin. "I need you downstairs in the small chapel for a wedding." He sighed and rubbed his chin again. "It's a strange situation. Right up your alley."

"What's that supposed to mean?" Myri crossed to the lockers. She hung up her coat and scarf and stared at her reflection in the small

13

mirror on the interior of the locker door. Using her fingers, she punked up short spikes of black hair, adding a thick styling gel to keep the spikes in place. Wide-set black eyes in an oval face stared back at her. She applied a light coat of lavender lipstick.

"It means sometimes you're a strange person… like this new haircut. What's that all about? Like just last week the key to the tap room jumped across the counter like a frog into your hand."

"I keep telling you. It wasn't magic." Myri massaged her hands. Most of the swelling and redness from the encounter with the semi-truck was gone. She wasn't sure what it was, but it wasn't magic. "Probably it was some small tremor from Mt. St. Helens."

Chris cocked his head. His eyebrows darted up in disbelief.

"So who'll be working in the Chapel with me? One of the twins?" she asked.

"No one, just you."

"Chris." She whirled around.

"Let me finish. I told you it was a bit strange." He stopped. The crease between his eyebrows deepened. "Maybe not strange, but different."

Myri shoved the locker door closed. "Whatever." She slipped the key into her pocket. "And I like my haircut. It's the new me, and I am not strange."

"Well, this wedding is. The bride's mother is Sylvia Dixon." He wrote the name down, tore the sheet from the clipboard, then handed it to her. "She has been the one making all the arrangements."

"Here, give that back." He put out his hand. "And this is the name of the bride and groom. According to the mom, the bride and groom are out of town and will be here in time for the wedding at two this afternoon."

"Is there a reception, or coffee or something afterwards that you want me to set up?"

"No. There are only supposed to be about ten people. That includes both sets of parents, the bride and groom and the minister. Mrs. Dixon wasn't sure how many would really come and she didn't explain."

"Well, what am I supposed to do?"

"Just help Mrs. Dixon. She called this morning and asked for you."

"I don't know any Mrs. Dixon. And how did she know I'd be here?"

"Well, she asked for a Myri."

"A Myri? How many Myris do you know?"

"She asked for Myri. You're Myri." Chris jutted his chin forward, his black eyes threatening. "I have to get the banquet hall ready for the Wine Society's Valentine's dinner. If you need anything, I'll be there."

Myri could tell from the change in the shape of his head and face that he was getting stressed. His head elongated and his cheekbones sharpened. Myri knew the shape shifting was neither permanent nor visible to others but an indication of some passing emotional or physical stress.

Myri smiled. "Don't worry. It'll work out."

CHAPTER THREE

A Wedding

The small chapel was downstairs at the south end of the Horse Heaven Winery. Myri put her ear to the crack between the double doors. When she heard nothing, she slowly opened them. Weak sunlight came through the floor-to-ceiling windows on her right. A simple altar arrangement, a wooden cross flanked by two white candles in pewter candlestick holders, sat on a narrow oak table on a low one-step up platform directly in front of her. Two links of black lattice divided the raised stage area from the seating area.

For a wedding just an hour away, the room seemed ill-prepared. There were no flowers. There were no ribbons. The seating area held ten chairs in one long row with a break in the middle, allowing a path to the altar. On the left, a small oak table was arranged at the end of the row away from the center pathway. Another small oval oak table that stood between the row of chairs and the lattice railing was bare.

This wedding evidently wasn't one of those over-planned, grueling family affairs where mothers and daughters, husbands and wives, his family, her family, and everyone in between, dueled it out until the minute "Here Comes the Bride" began. But the austerity of decoration seemed an extreme reaction to the anxiety of wedding planning.

The room was small, meant to hold up to fifteen people at most, and the air had the stale, musty smell of a closed damp place like a root cellar. She went back to prop open the doors. She scanned the hallway, thinking that she heard footsteps, but saw no one.

Back in the room, she walked to the windows that faced a pond ringed by a cement pathway. Large, empty clay pots sat at intervals along the path. Past the pond, a frosted mat of lawn spread to the foot of the wintering vineyard where row upon row of skeletal wiring waited for the hibernating gray stumps to put out green shoots.

"Myri?" Myri jumped. "I'm Sylvia Dixon."

Myri came forward and reached for the outstretched hand. Her first impressions of the woman were contrasts. The hand was soft but at the same time steady. The face was ivory, smooth and relaxed, but with a firm chin. A Grecian high-bridged nose separated large eyes, one brown, one blue.

"Can I help you with that?" Myri pointed to a brown briefcase Mrs. Dixon held. "Or are there other things in the car that I can go get?"

"No." Mrs. Dixon set the bag gently on the floor. She surveyed the room. "I think I have everything we're going to need."

Nothing about the woman was familiar to Myri: not the expertly swept up French roll of honey blond hair nor the finely drawn eyebrows or the carefully applied makeup. The brown tweed suit was definitely retro, out of the sixties, something Jackie Kennedy might have worn. The jacket flared briefly at the waist over her hips. Myri was sure that the collar and the trim were real mink, that if she touched the fur, it would roll supple and rich between her fingers.

"Do I know you?" Myri asked. Nobody she knew would ever wear real fur.

"No, I don't think so." Mrs. Dixon smiled. Her lips rode up into a broad smile — a wide mobile mouth more in tune with the mismatched eyes than the patrician nose.

An unusual face, an unusual person, Myri decided, disguised in an elegant conservative suit.

"We can talk later." Mrs. Dixon checked her watch. "Right now, would you mind going upstairs to wait for the minister. Her name is Sharon Dramis and you won't miss her. She's shorter even than you, a very petite blonde. I'll take care of what needs to be done in here."

"Is there anyone else I should look for?" Like a father, a groom, a bride? Myri ticked them off to herself.

"My husband might come," Mrs. Dixon said, "but he knows his way down."

Did Chris say this wedding was different? His first description, strange, seemed better.

Upstairs, the luau-clad tourists from the van were singing the Hawaiian Wedding Song. Arm-in-arm they filed out the front door wedged open by the tour guide – the woman in the red muumuu. She played the ukulele as oblivious to the arctic draft created by the open door as the revelers.

Myri jerked to a stop. The tour guide was Ruby. When their eyes met, Ruby raised the uke in salute and released the doors following the departing group.

"Are you here to help?" Stella, one of the twins servicing the bar, called out. "We could use it." She waved a hand toward the counter littered with dirty glasses. Myri knew it was Stella because she was dressed all in black. Stephenia, the other twin, dressed in flashy neon colors, which today was tangerine. Without the color preferences the two girls would have been impossible to tell apart. Both were hearty and well-built with long auburn ponytails, alert blue eyes and wide cheekbones.

"No, I'm waiting for the minister for the wedding downstairs." Myri headed toward the fifteen foot oversized fireplace at the far end of the room.

"Lucky you," Stella said as Myri passed by. "They left a real mess."

"I don't suppose anyone got sick," Myri asked, "or anything?" Why else would Ruby be here, except to help a dying person to the other side? Evidently she wasn't staying for the wedding. "Did they look sick?"

Stella shook her head. "No." She hoisted an empty glass canister. "They even ate all the breadsticks. Can you believe that?"

Myri's backside was just getting toasty when the front doors heaved inward. A tall brown-skinned man, wearing a gaudy teal shirt imprinted with orange whales, braced one of the doors open with his shoulder while helping a woman – surely the expected pastor – through the opening.

"She slipped on the stones outside," the man said. He escorted the petite blonde to Myri. "Ruby said you were waiting for her. I'm Samson, Ruby's driver."

When the man smiled, Myri caught her breath. His kind, melted chocolate eyes reminded her of Michael Gilbert, her middle school true love – a husky Mexican boy with a gentle nature. He came to school only a few weeks before joining his family in the asparagus fields.

"I'm Myri. You remind me of someone."

"Michael? He's a great kid."

"You know him?" Myri glanced at the pastor, not sure of how much to say. "Are you…" Myri couldn't decide how to ask him. The pastor probably believed in spirits, but perhaps not spirits on wine tours dressed in splashy Hawaiian shirts with orange whales.

"Am I late? Yes I am," Samson said. He signaled a thanks with a thumb-to-finger circle. To the pastor he said: "You're in good hands. Myri's here to show you the way."

"It's this way." Myri pointed down the hallway. "Can I take your coat?"

"Not yet. I'm still cold." Pastor Dramis turned around. "Thanks, Samson." But he was already gone. "A nice young man. He seemed to know exactly what I needed."

"Did you twist your ankle?" Myri asked.

"I'm fine. This weather is just miserable. My hands are chapped, my lips are chapped. I hate this bitter cold."

"Hi, Sharon." Mrs. Dixon waited at the bottom of the stairs. She rummaged around in the brown bag. "Here try some of this." She pulled out a tube of hand lotion.

"Hi, Sylvia. I will."

"You too, Myri?"

"Sure, thanks." Myri rubbed the lavender scented oil in her palms. Both the pastor and Mrs. Dixon were at ease and seemed to know what was going on, even if no one else did.

"Now you can take this."

Myri carried the pastor's coat to an alcove next to the small chapel. When she returned, they were inside. Myri waited at the back near the doors.

Mrs. Dixon had made a few adjustments while Myri was gone. The candles were now lit. Two five-by-seven pictures were angled in a "V" on the small oak table between the railing and the row of chairs. The table on the left at the end of the row had a CD player on it, battery-operated evidently, as Myri didn't see any cord. The path leading up to the altar was scattered with rose petals.

Pastor Dramis, in formal clerical robes, positioned herself next to the small table in front.

The clock on the wall read one fifty-five. There was still no bride or groom; there was one mother, no fathers, no bridesmaid, and no groomsmen.

Mrs. Dixon placed a small wreath of miniature yellow roses and Baby's Breath in the angle between the two photos.

"Are we ready?" the pastor asked. She turned to Mrs. Dixon, who sat on a chair in the row on the left, next to the table with the CD player.

"Myri, will you close the doors and sit there?" Mrs. Dixon pointed to the first chair in the row on the right nearest the pastor. When Myri settled, Mrs. Dixon hit the play button on the CD player. The familiar sound of Wagner's Bridal Chorus began. Myri sang "Here Comes the Bride" in her head while stealing a quick glance at the door. When Mrs. Dixon stood, Myri stood, not sure what to do with her hands. They were throbbing, strong and steady as heartbeats.

The candles flickered once in the still room and then flickered again. The rose petals stirred, shifting side to side. When Mrs. Dixon switched off the CD player, the candles righted into steady flames. Myri could smell the hot wax and the sweet scent of roses.

"Please sit," the pastor instructed. Myri edged back in the chair but sat alert, watching Mrs. Dixon from the corner of her eye.

"Dearly beloved, we are gathered here, in the presence of God and this company, to unite Karen Elaine Dixon and Randall Ernest Delany." The pastor recited from memory, staring confidently at the empty space directly in front of her.

Myri drew in a long breath, waiting for the next part and knowing how important a question it was.

"Who gives this woman?"

Myri felt rather than heard the doors open. A current of air swept through the room, scattering rose petals as a man made his way to stand beside Mrs. Dixon.

"I do," he said, reaching for his wife's hand.

Bald head, blue suit, not as tall as his wife, was all Myri could tell of the man.

The ritual continued, each part enunciated with appropriate pauses to allow for responses, but Myri heard none.

"I now pronounce you husband and wife." The pastor ended with a smile, and then made a blessing sign over the wreath on the oak table.

Mrs. Dixon pushed the CD. Mendelssohn's "The Wedding March" filled the room.

Next came the sound of satin against satin, a rustling down the path over the remaining rose petals. The candles fluttered and went out.

Pastor Dramis picked up the wreath and followed Mr. and Mrs. Dixon to the doors, where all three turned to face the altar. The Pastor stretched out her hands, letting the wreath lay flat in them as if on a tray.

"Myri," Mrs. Dixon said, "get ready, the bride is going to throw the bouquet."

Myri stood and stepped forward. Her forehead wrinkled in confusion but her hands rose, palms up, until they were at waist level.

The wreath came up and off the Pastor's hands in slow motion, turning like a lazy Frisbee around and around, crossing the space to land gently in Myri's.

Myri felt the throbbing in her palms fade and cool even as the scent of rose and baby's breath engulfed her. She raised the flowers closer to her face and inhaled.

Imagine me catching the bridal bouquet. Well, not exactly catching, she decided, more like receiving. But not exactly that either as the Pastor had not thrown the bouquet.

Strange, definitely, but Myri felt a flood of joy flash through her. And the Pastor and the Dixons were smiling at her.

"Myri, will you bring the things out to me? In the satchel is fine," Mrs. Dixon said. She leaned her head onto Mr. Dixon's shoulder. He was still holding her hand.

The gray day had brightened. Weak rays of a February sun lingering in winter's Southwestern sky made shadows on the walls. Myri went to the pictures on the table. One was an engagement shot for the newspaper: a typical photo of the smiling couple. The other was not a picture but a framed obituary notice.

The bride and groom had been killed instantly on the way to the Blue Mountain Ski Resort only one week before their wedding, February 14th, one year earlier.

Myri touched the two frames to her heart before stowing them on top of the CD player in the satchel. She slipped the wreath on her wrist.

Once outside Myri handed the satchel to Mr. Dixon.

Myri unstrung the wreath from her wrist, presenting it in both hands to Mrs. Dixon.

"Oh no, that's yours." Mrs. Dixon pointed to the flowers. "Ruby left it for you."

"Ruby?" Myri hesitated. "Oh, that Ruby." She nodded. "But I don't even have a boyfriend. Alive or dead." Myri blushed. "I am so sorry."

Mrs. Dixon glanced tenderly at Mr. Dixon. "Things change," she said.

Myri agreed silently. Things did change. All the time. But what did Mrs. Dixon mean? Was change coming for Myri or had change already come because Mr. Dixon came to the wedding?

CHAPTER FOUR

Snow and Ice

Myri held the phone at arm's length.

"Chris, honestly I would come in if I could." She brought the phone closer to her ear once he stopped yelling. "I've got an exam today and an interview in Walla Walla. It's really important to me, a chance to get into the Culinary Arts Program at the Community College."

She listened to Chris mutter his way from anxious need to concerned friendship.

"Yes, I'll be careful," Myri said. "I know the roads are terrible, but I have snow tires on. I'll go slow. Why don't you try one of the twins? They need the work as much as I do."

Things change, Mrs. Dixon had said. Myri hoped so. She couldn't go on working two jobs at minimum wage and make ends meet. The twelve hundred square foot modular home on the acre of land her dad left her was free of debt. That helped, but it didn't pay the utility bills, the insurance or the taxes. He hadn't left much else, except a beat up 1950 green Ford pick-up he'd claimed was worth its weight in gold. So far no one had come knocking at her door to buy the antique pick-up truck. It had sat idle in the shop since his death. Myri needed a career that would provide a decent income, and something she could get passionate about, like food.

As soon as she hung up the phone, she made a quick dash into the bathroom to brush her teeth, wash her face and to perk up short spiky lengths of her black hair with gel. She added a thin layer of lavender lipstick and took one last look at herself in the full length mirror. Black pants, black turtleneck. She had dressed the part of the creative artist – someone serious about perfection. She smiled at herself. Made a happy face. Her black eyes responded, sparkling excitement.

At the front door she jerked a black puffy ski jacket from the closet: a great bargain from the thrift shop at only $5. The long shaggy crocheted scarf she wound around her neck was another second-hand treasure. The thick gray gloves clipped together and hanging over the door knob, she ignored. Her hands were already warm.

The forty minutes she allotted for the trip were not enough. Although the four lane road was cleared, the newly fallen snow ploughed to the sides, the radio warned of black ice. Traffic crawled along under thirty miles an hour in the rutted, more traveled right hand lane. She took a deep breath and queued up behind a white Toyota Camry, leaving what she hoped was enough room in case of an unexpected mishap.

A red suburban raced up behind her, traveling well over the speed limit. She caught a glimpse of it in the mirror. Her stomach lurched. She was sure it was going to rear end her, but instead it zagged into the left lane moments before impact and passed her. It pirouetted a three-sixty circle as the driver pulled back into the right lane in front of her, slid off the pavement, bounced off the bank and thudded to a stop.

Myri tapped the brakes gently. After a slow slide to a stop, she threw open the door, tested the icy road, then got out. Smoke billowed from under the suburban's crunched hood. She tried to run, fell, got up and tried again.

"Hey girlie, get out of the road!" a man yelled from a blue pick-up truck that pulled up beside her. "You're gonna get killed."

Myri stepped towards the bank, unaware she had been standing in the middle of the road. The man parked the truck behind her car.

"Get back," he said. As he lifted a fire extinguisher from behind his seat, the suburban burst into flames.

Myri stared at the rising thick, acrid smoke that choked and seared her lungs. The man advanced and flooded the hood and the windshield of the suburban with white foam.

Traffic inched by in the left lane. A green BMW stopped. The passenger window came down and a gray-haired woman poked her head out.

"We've called 911," she said. The window went up and the car moved slowly forward.

Myri stood useless, her heart racing. The driver of the pick-up retreated, coughing and gagging, shielding his nose and mouth with a red bandana.

"Someone called for help." Myri glanced back and forth, first at the burning vehicle and then at the fire extinguisher. "Shouldn't we be doing something? How about the people inside?"

The man rolled his lips into a tight line. "Can't do no more."

A white stretch limo with a purple and green logo of clustering grapes on the side pulled in behind the smoldering vehicle. Signage on the side advertised "Desert Imp Wine Tours."

A man in a bulky silver coat got out of the driver side. A purple ski hat was pulled down, covering his ears and most of his forehead. He stepped back to open the rear door.

Myri knew it was Ruby even before the spirit exited the car. The red gauzy caftan and the long flowing black hair were all that Myri needed to see. If Ruby was here, the pick up's driver was right, no more could be done. The rest was up to Ruby.

"You think it'd be all right if I left?" Myri asked. "I have an appointment in Walla Walla."

"You go on," the pick-up driver said. "No use both of us standing here in the cold. That guy was driving way too fast. He passed me about a mile back. Stupid kids don't know nothing about black ice." He wiped his face with the kerchief and put it back into his hip pocket. "I'll wait till the police come. I'm retired. Ain't got nothing else to do except take my old Aunt Tillie for a ride"

"Thanks." Myri studied the man, conscious for the first time of his heavy laced-up work boots and rust brown Carhartt overalls. His eyes were rheumy blue and red-rimmed. Gray stubble speckled his cheeks. "If you hadn't yelled at me, I might have been seriously hurt."

"Don't never know, do we, what's going to happen?" He waved her away.

CHAPTER FIVE

Walla Walla

The rest of the drive was slow. She would be too late for the interview but maybe in time to take the exam. The trip wouldn't be a total waste.

At the Main Street exit she veered right, taking the ramp into downtown Walla Walla. She moved into the left lane at the first opportunity, to prepare for the left onto University Avenue. She flicked the left turn signal down and waited for an oncoming car to pass. Both her hands started to pulse rapidly. When she tried to rotate the wheel for the turn, it stuck. Despite her intention, her hands rotated the wheel in the opposite direction. Her yellow Honda Civic merged into the right lane.

Myri checked the rearview mirror. The driver behind her had every right to be angry as she crowded him out, but he eased back with no honking complaint and no menacing hand gestures.

"What is going on? This is totally not the right time," Myri said. "Later, after the test. I'll have all day. It can't be more important than my future."

At the next light, with both hands stuck to the wheel on each side, she made a wide gliding right, just missing a snow bank barricading the sidewalk. Two more blocks brought her to the Goodwill Thrift store. The parking lot on the west side was minimally ploughed, the parking slots reduced by half.

"You won. Now what?" Myri asked. Her hands, now released from the wheel, settled in her lap. "Can we make this quick, whatever it is?"

Except for the jangling of the bell attached to the door that announced her entry, the store was quiet. Myri began a methodical walk, going down each aisle, her hands dangled along her thighs, palms out.

She worked her way past a row of shoes, wrinkling her nose at the sweaty foot smell, and then a rack of winter coats with scruffy fur collars. There was a tumble of different sized baskets in a large round bin.

"This could take all day." She marched past a grouping of prom dresses and bridal gowns. "Snap it up."

"Can I help you find something?" The voice came from behind her.

"No, just looking," Myri said without turning around. "Come on, come on," she muttered to herself. "I don't have all day." Her hands hung hot and limp without response until she got to the housewares section, then they pulsed wildly.

"I don't need another casserole dish." She tapped her boots against the hard gray linoleum floor. "All this for another pan? Give me a break."

"Are you sure I can't help you, miss?" An elderly woman in a faded blue calico smock with two deep front pockets came around the counter to face her. She tipped her head to one side.

"Nope, talking to myself, just looking." Myri smiled.

"Well, ring the bell at the checkout counter when you're ready. We're in the back pricing some new items."

"Sure thing." Myri watched the woman retreat, waiting until she was out of sight before edging closer to the shelving.

Her feet stuck to the floor in front of a row of plates and saucers. She reached out her hands until she felt a definite tug and then waited to see if anything moved. A six-inch plate inched to the edge of the shelf. She picked it up. In the foreground a train, its boxcars painted in bright childish crayon colors – green, yellow, blue – crossed a trestle bridge. The chugging black engine spewed puffs of gray smoke. Ducks and geese and cows were sprinkled through the landscape. At the very bottom, a tiny shepherd with a staff stood in the middle of a herd of sheep. She turned the plate over and saw $3.29 – a price she could afford.

"Done," she whispered. She lifted her right foot, testing to make sure she could move, and then her left. "Let's go."

As she made her way to the cash register, she felt a wave of heat from her hands through her arms sweep across her torso and into her heart like the jab of an arrow.

She tapped the silver bell at the checkout. Two women came out of the back. One was the woman in the calico smock. She waved the other woman back.

"I'll handle this, Ellie," she said, sticking the pencil she carried into a gray-haired bun swept up to sit on the top of her head.

"So you found a treasure after all. We just marked this and put it out. Let me wrap it up for you."

"No, thanks. I'm in a hurry." Myri laid four dollars on the counter. "Keep the change." She stuffed the plate safely inside her purse and left the store, headed for the car as fast as she could on the slippery pavement.

"Later," she said, "I'll figure it out later, after my test."

CHAPTER SIX

A Gilbert

Myri ran down the hall and slid to a stop in front of the desk. The proctor sitting in front of Room 346A looked up from her book.

"I'm here to take the 10:30 exam for the Culinary Institute Program."

The proctor rolled her wrist over, showing Myri not only a watch but a Celtic love knots tattoo on her upper arm.

"You're too late. It already started." The young woman pushed a brochure towards Myri. "You'll have to reschedule."

"I'm just a few minutes late. I came all the way from the Tri-Cities and the roads are terrible."

"Sorry. The doors closed at 10:30 AM." The proctor shrugged and went back to her book.

Myri swung around, clutched her purse and muttered to herself all the way back down the hall. In a fit of frustration and self-pity she kicked at the legs of a small brown leather couch arranged near the doors in a small alcove.

She dropped onto the couch and brought her hands up to her face.

"And now what? Do you know how much I wanted this opportunity? I can't count on anyone but me. I'm an only child, remember, without parents?" Her dad had refused to go back to the Midwest to see his family and they, in response, hadn't come to see him or his daughter. Myri knew little about her mother's side.

"She was a gypsy, your ma," her dad had said. "She liked them big hoop earrings and made the best strawberry shortcake a man could ever want." He'd considered that enough said.

A man in a dark brown suit, tan shirt and yellow polka dot bow tie came down the hall and stopped in front of her.

"Are you okay?" He had a full beard, well-trimmed but more gray than the rusty color of his hair. Myri smelled pipe smoke. The pipe itself jutted out of the pocket of his jacket. His sea-green eyes watched her with interest. He was probably one of the professors she would never have.

"It's nothing. Just ranting to myself." She reached inside her bag to scrounge for a piece of tissue. The plate came out first, and she laid it on the seat beside her. "I've just had a bad morning." The man bent down to examine the plate.

"Is that a Gilbert?" He reached for it.

"A what?" Myri sniffled and wiped her nose.

"May I?" He picked up the plate. After studying it, he turned it over. "Yes. It is. I thought it was by the little guy in the corner." He turned the plate back over. "See this shepherd in the middle of the sheep? It's his signature."

"Is it valuable?" Maybe that was the answer. The plate was a rare antique, so valuable that it would pay her way through college. Her hands weren't so dumb after all.

"Some of them are. It depends on the series. The ones he painted in Japan are more collectors' items than the recent ones. You can check him out on line: Michael Gilbert." He tapped the back of the plate. "There's a number on the back."

"What did you say his name was?"

"Interestingly enough, he used to be one of my students. I heard he went into the Navy, bummed around Asia for a while." He handed her the plate. "This one's an interesting piece. He loved locomotives. That's what you paid for it, $3.29?" he asked. "You got a bargain. Most of them are in the twenty to thirty dollar range. You should keep it. Start your own collection."

"Michael Gilbert?" Myri sat up, taking the plate and stuffing the Kleenex in her pocket. "I used to know a Michael Gilbert. About my age, mid-twenties? I went to school with him in Pasco."

"I think he's a bit older, but I'm not sure."

She studied the shepherd. He didn't look Mexican like the boy she remembered in middle school. But a shepherd watches out for the flock, which was like Michael. He kept an eye on his younger brothers and sisters, the ones old enough to come to school. Samson had called Michael a nice kid. Myri called him brave. He was a husky boy with large, rich-chocolate eyes. After a few weeks in school, he'd left to help his family in the fields during the asparagus harvest. He was bigger than most of her classmates. He was older too, but it wasn't his size or his eyes that captured her admiration; it was his quiet courage.

One day at recess, a group of boys circled Judy Weston who had come to school so proud of her new gray Pendleton skirt with a hand appliquéd white poodle on it.

"Arf, arf," the boys had sniped, "a dog skirt for a dog of a girl," until Michael moved into the ring to stand beside Judy, then the boys had backed away, but not without a parting sneer.

"Guess we know what kind of girls these wetbacks like."

Michael had escorted Judy back to the school building.

"Yes, I think I know him," Myri said.

"Well, if you find him, tell him to call me." The man drew a business card from his wallet. "I bet we could find a position for him."

She studied the card before replying. "Thanks, Professor Canton. I can't imagine that I'll ever see him again, especially if he's famous." Myri handed the card back to him. "It was just an accident I found the plate."

He shook his head. "I sometimes think accident is just another word for Fate."

CHAPTER SEVEN

Valentine

Myri worked on the pea patch. A flock of crows gathered in the wintering sycamore nearby to caw and to bounce their heads in loud approval of her digging. The worms she turned over were sluggish, easy pickings in the chill March air. The crows, eager for her to leave the scene so they could feast, jumped from limb to limb, fluttered their wings and kept up bossy comments.

"You guys are way too noisy," Myri shouted at them. "Just wait your turn. I'm getting peas in the ground before April this year. You hear me?"

When the sun came out from behind a cloud the day was moderately warm, one of the first days of broken sunshine after two weeks of mournful, gray overcast skies.

"Hey, kiddo, who're you talking to?"

Myri, startled, rested the hoe in the trench she'd just dug with the Little Wonder tiller and turned to face the man coming along the path.

"Al. I didn't hear the gate." She recognized his barrel chest, which he pushed forward like a spinnaker full of wind, and his distinctive side-to-side gait on stubby legs. A teal colored Mariner's stocking cap, which he wore year round, was pulled down to cover his ears. He was no fashion statement, but looked warm in a royal blue flannel shirt under a pair of striped black and white overalls.

She didn't recognize the man following him – taller by six inches and bareheaded. His caramel-colored cashmere coat and polished brown tasseled loafers were expensive and made for city sidewalks. His progress was slower than Al's and more cautious as he put one foot in front of the other with obvious distaste, avoiding an occasional muddy bald spot along a beaten down mat of soggy grass that passed for a path from the front gate to the garden.

"Hey, what brings you way out here and on a Sunday? Come to help me plant peas? Talk to the crows? That's about all that's going on."

"Heck no." Al stopped in front of her, a big pumpkin grin on his face.

Harmless, Myri's dad had said of Al. To which she had added, "And a bit slow."

"Don't get smart, young lady," her dad had frowned. "Lots of things you don't know nothing about."

To avoid any more of her dad's disapproval, she'd kept the last comment to herself, "and way too much meth," which she did know something about, having spent a summer working in the cafeteria at the Court House listening to the raw talk of drug users and drug busters.

"I just got to thinking about you and your dad." Al's cheerfulness disappeared. He rubbed the right toe of his black heavy work boot against a clump of grass. "Wondered if you needed anything?"

"Thanks, that's awfully kind of you," she said. "But I'm getting along."

"This is a nice place he left you." Al brightened. "Where's the old mutt?"

He looked around, searching the small strip of grass around the doublewide manufactured home, then shifted his head to look over her, searching the half-acre behind the garden space.

"Out in the shop?" He motioned to the ten by twenty foot metal outbuilding set in the north corner of the lot.

"I had to put her down."

"Oh, too bad." Al bobbed his head. "We wasn't sure you was home. Didn't see no car."

"It's behind the shop near the wood pile."

"Kind of lonely out here, ain't it?"

"The crows and coyotes keep me company," Myri said. "And the neighbors down the road have dogs a plenty that seem to find their way here."

"This here is Johnny Valentine." Al thumbed an introduction to the man who had followed him.

Valentine stood with both hands deep in his coat pockets. When he moved closer, Myri could see the burgundy plaid muffler wrapped around his neck, its ends tucked into his coat.

"He knew your dad from way back, when they was just kids." Al bobbed his head again, agreeing with himself that he had the information right.

"Johnny Valentine?" Her eyebrows shot up. "Really? I never heard Dad talk about anyone named Valentine." She slid off the blue cotton garden gloves she wore, more for protection against blisters than for warmth. She stuffed the gloves into the pockets of her gray sleeveless fleece.

"You're a long way from home if you knew my dad as a kid. All the way from Missouri."

"Kansas City, actually. We hooked up in Kansas City." Valentine brought his right hand, encased in a fawn colored driving glove, slowly out of the coat pocket.

Myri noted the small gold fastening knob on the back. Real leather, but too thin to supply protection from the cold. More for style, or protection of another sort.

Although Valentine faced her, she noticed the way his pale brown eyes darted around, paying more attention to the area around her and behind her than to her.

Myri extended her hand. Their hands almost met. She wasn't sure what happened, two things at once. Her palm was repelled as if by a magnetic force and a dog came from behind Valentine and ploughed into her. She spun sideways and dropped to her knees.

"Zoe," Myri shouted at the gray and white wolfhound. The dog whirled away, danced around her and then stopped to sniff the two men. Zoe emitted a low growl. As she backed away, her lips inched up. She bared her teeth and snarled.

"Hey, now," Al said, "is she dangerous?"

"No." Myri pushed herself up. "She's just a puppy and full of herself." She tugged at Zoe's collar but couldn't budge her. Valentine's hand slipped back into his pocket.

"I don't like dogs," Valentine said. His eyes shifted. The pupils contracted as he focused on Zoe.

Myri stroked Zoe's head but she watched Valentine's hand.

He might have a gun in his pocket. Some of her dad's pals from the past were on the slightly shady side of the law. They had their own set of rules about right and wrong. Until she knew different, she'd respect Zoe's evaluation.

"I'll put her in the house and walk her home later."

When Myri returned, the two men weren't on the lawn. They had moved past the garden towards the shop.

"How about a cup of tea?" she asked coming up behind them, hoping that the offer would be too womanish for them to accept.

"Naw, we gotta go. I just wanted Johnny to see your dad's place, since he used to know him. Your dad was always proud of this place, his shop." Al waved toward the building.

Valentine turned around. "You look a lot like your mom. A gypsy or an Indian, wasn't she? Something like that?"

"Something like that." Myri didn't like his hard inquisitive stare. His eyes hadn't improved in warmth once Zoe was out of the way. He still carried his hands in his pockets.

"I heard your dad did real good," he said. "He was always good with his hands. Had one of those photo memories. Heard he did real good. "

"That so?" Myri waved her hand. "Here's his domain, what he left."

"How about his old green truck? You still got it?" Al asked.

"It's in the shop. I had it towed and haven't gotten around to even cleaning it out yet."

"What happened?" Al puckered his lips and shook his head. "He was so careful with that old truck, practically lived in it."

"Police think that he dozed off at the wheel, hit the guard rail. Bashed himself up and the side of the truck."

"Good," Valentine echoed. "Yeah, I heard he did real good."

"They should call you Johnny one-note," Myri said. At five three, she didn't come up to Valentine's shoulder, but she inched forward as she spoke.

Valentine shrugged and twitched his neck and shoulders as if tossing off a pesky fly.

"Yeah, you're a funny girl," he said. It wasn't approval he sent her way but a grimace that pulled down the edges of his wide face and set the angle of his lips in a scowl.

Myri recognized the cause of his menacing stare. Too much lip from a pipsqueak female.

He was a dangerous man, of that Myri was certain. His fleshy cheeks sagged over his jaw line like a bulldog and a scar that pulled down his left eyelid was proof enough he wasn't afraid of a fight. The expensive clothes couldn't disguise a brutal insistence to have things his way whatever the cost.

"Johnny, I think we ought to go." Al rubbed his nose.

"Like my dad used to say, come back when you can't stay so long," Myri said, widening her stance and crossing her arms over her chest. Never give in to a bully. A lesson she'd learned from Michael Gilbert.

"Yeah, you're a funny girl," Valentine said.

"Ha, ha," Al blew out. "We got that meeting at the garage, remember." He tapped Valentine on the sleeve.

"Shut your trap, Al," Valentine snapped. "Go get in the car."

Al hung his head and took a couple of steps back before turning to head for a silver Lincoln

Town car parked beside the six-foot-high chain link fence separating Myri's narrow lawn from the gravel road.

"You ever decide you want to sell your dad's pick-up, let me know. Al told me all about it, a Ford, fifties model. I'm a collector."

"I'll think about it," she said. "It has sentimental value."

"Sentimental can't buy much, except trouble."

"What else do you collect?" she asked. "I just bought a plate you might like."

The plate was worth about thirty dollars, as the professor predicted. Myri had done some research on line. She even looked up Gilbert in the phone book, thinking that he might have returned to the area. Many immigrant families put down roots in the Columbia Basin. There were over twenty individual Gilberts listed and several businesses – mostly auto repair shops – and one Gilberto, but no Michael Gilbert. She didn't remember the name of any of the younger Gilbert siblings.

"Don't smart mouth me." Valentine leaned in. "When you decide that old truck is too much trouble, let me know."

Myri watched him skirt the muddy patches. He went through and then latched the gate.

When he turned and looked back, seven of the crows from the sycamore tree rose in unison. They settled in ominous silence in a row along the top of the fence and faced the road.

A cloud swept in front of the sun and just as quickly scudded past. Myri felt the change in temperature: the cold as the cloud moved to hide the sun, the warmth as the cloud passed. But what she noticed most as sunlight became shade and sunlight again was Valentine's energy field. Dots and dashes of fluctuating energy arched over him, not to him, not through but around him.

In Myri's world that could only mean one thing. Valentine was dead. How was he therefore breathing, watching her? Was he dead or alive?

As the questions tumbled through her mind, a US Mail delivery truck came around the Lincoln and pulled up to Myri's mailbox near the gate. Myri saw a hand come out with a piece of mail, followed by a brown face with flowing black hair and just a glimpse of red shimmer. Ruby poked a letter inside the box and refastened the latch.

The mail truck went on down the road. The Lincoln made a hard U-turn, spitting gravel behind the tires. Myri kept an eye on the Lincoln until it disappeared over the railroad tracks and dropped into the gulley on the other side then she fetched Zoe from the house.

"Let's get you back home to LuAnn."

Zoe dashed for the fence and made a lunge for the crows only to hit the fence breast high and bounce back. The crows, with unconcerned ease, lifted up to reconvene in the sycamore tree.

"You numb nut. Take it easy. You're not big enough or fast enough to catch crows."

Myri opened the gate.

Zoe charged through and raced down the road.

Myri gave up. She decided to give LuAnn a call after fetching the mail. Zoe would probably be back in her own yard by then.

Myri was interested in what Ruby left. Perhaps it was an explanation about Valentine. What kind of life form had no energy field? Why did her hand repel his? Or did his hand repel hers? Was he dangerous, a threat to her or to everyone and everything, a being not dead but not truly alive?

CHAPTER EIGHT

An Invitation

The mail wasn't a letter and it wasn't from Ruby. The mailbox contained one thick cream-colored envelope addressed to Ms. Myri Elena Wolfen. Inside the envelope was a card, wheat colored, made of hand-crafted paper. The front was embossed with a bright yellow kite with a tail of colored ribbons. A black string went sideways across the card's face and disappeared over the edge. When Myri opened the card, the string continued to the lower right and was held by a little girl with copper colored pigtails and wearing a pink ruffled pinafore.

Dear Myri, the note began, *I just wanted to tell you again how much your help at Karen and Randy's wedding meant to me and Mr. Dixon. I believe you could be of great help to a friend of mine. Her name is Rose*

Burton. She lives on the coast near Seaview, not too far from Ilwaco where I live. I told her to call you. When she calls I hope you will say yes. I would be happy to pay for your room at the Claiborne. Regards, Sylvia Dixon

Rose Burton had been hesitant on the phone when she called. She said she trusted Mrs. Dixon's instincts and wondered if Myri could come to Seaview on the last Sunday of the month. Rose didn't want to say any more on the phone. She said she preferred to wait and speak with Myri in person.

The Long Beach Peninsula where Mrs. Dixon lived had two great lures: Fresh Pacific oysters and the Claiborne Inn. The Claiborne had a statewide reputation for the best Northwest cuisine. Mrs. Dixon's offer to pay her lodging for one night if she decided to come was an offer not to be refused. After Myri called to make sure the Claiborne was open in the off-season, she petitioned both her employers for time off. Sunday was her regular day off. Chris gave her Saturday and Sol agreed to a half day on Monday.

CHAPTER NINE

The Claiborne

A west wind coming off the ocean whipped the flag in front of the tourist information kiosk. Ominous black-bellied clouds hovered on the horizon. Myri hoped to beat the storm. She made the right turn onto Pacific Ave., the main road through Seaview. March was not a busy month for Long Beach Peninsula towns. High time was July through Labor Day but even then the Pacific Ocean was cold and dangerous along this northerly stretch of coastline. In early spring only the determined few braved the cold winds, the rain, and the gloomy weather for the sporadic razor clam digging weekends allowed by the State Park Service. Some, passionate about Willapa Bay oysters, came to eat their fill at affordable prices.

This Saturday no tourists shuffled along the streets with their kids in tow. No one juggled buckets and shovels and ice cream cones. No festive kites zigzagged the sky. The go-cart track was closed.

Myri glanced again at the MapQuest directions. The Claiborne had to be close and on the left. Since no one was behind her, she slowed to a crawl. She noted that the signs in dark, dusty windows alternated between Closed for the Winter and Going Out of Business. A 24-hour food mart was open as well as the Train Station Tavern next to it. Flashing neon signs in the tavern advertised The Best Barbecue Shrimp.

Her mouth watered. It was after one, long past her normal lunchtime. The drive from Longview over the curvy two-lane highway was beautiful but frustrating. When the patches of fog and mist that curled around the tall pines along the Columbia River lifted enough to make good time, she was delayed behind slow moving logging trucks.

At the light she realized that she must have missed the Inn. She took the next left to circle back. The paved road quickly turned to dirt and dumped onto the beach. Strong winds and a pounding tide raised ridges of whitecaps. She pulled to the edge of the road and rolled down the window.

She was glad just to be on the beach, to hear the surf, to smell the salt. That would be reward enough for the long trip, that and the great food, but she hoped she could help Mrs. Dixon and her friend as well.

She dipped her chin to her chest and forced her shoulder down in a good stretch before she made a U-turn. At the stop sign she went right and kept a slow pace. She spotted the Claiborne, a two story rambling house, set back from the street, painted iron gray, white trimmed, and surrounded by a low hedge. A four-car parking lot on the north side faced a handicapped ramp.

She followed the ramp from the parking lot along the side of the building to the front. The buttery aroma that hit her when she opened the door made her smile.

No one responded when she tapped the bell at the front desk. From her right in the dining room came the jumbled clattering sounds of plates and bowls and laughter. The bar was just opposite the formal dining area and on her left. She went to its swinging half double doors and craned her neck over to see inside. Eight small tables stood in the curve of a large bay window and arched around a central U-shaped counter. Wine glasses hung in glistening rows above the central section. A bartender, casually dressed in blue jeans and denim shirt, was busy twisting a corkscrew. He waved her in.

"Please come in. You're just in time for the last bowl of chowder." He extracted the cork with a flourish and held it out for Myri to sniff. "You can't beat this Satin Creek Chardonnay." He pointed to a table in front of a stained glass window picturing a string-legged sandpiper on the beach. Above the sandpiper, high in an azure sky, gulls glided, aloft on wide stretched wings.

Myri pulled out a chair. "I'm supposed to meet someone in the lobby at two."

"My name's Neil." The bartender slid a wineglass with a tasting portion of the chardonnay in front of her. "What do you think of this?"

"I'm Myri." She picked up the glass and swirled the liquid, and then raised it to her nose. "Nice nose." She sipped. "Nice taste."

"Good, because all I have left is a bowl of salmon chowder and this wine is what you need with it, that and a few crackers." He poured a generous portion, more than the usual four ounces.

"Great." Myri scooted up to the table. "But before I leave I want to try your country pâté."

"I'm so sorry. The pâté we have at the moment is for the wine maker dinner tonight.

Are you staying with us? Do you want to come? A five course meal with a paired wine for only seventy-five dollars a person."

"I am staying the night, but that's a little outside my budget, thanks anyway." What also wasn't in her budget was a glass of wine at lunch.

"I'll get the chowder."

"Make it a cup instead of a bowl," Myri said.

Neil returned carrying a tray loaded with a white ceramic tureen with lid, a soup bowl and a basket of crackers.

"That's a cup?" Myri stared at the tureen.

"Beans, he's the chef, says, 'eat what you want.'" Neil backed away from the table after depositing the dishes. He wiped the soup spoon with an extravagant motion and then placed it on her right with a crisp white napkin. "We make our own crackers. These are cracked pepper."

"Thanks." Myri lifted the lid of the tureen. "It smells wonderful."

"Please, dig in." He stepped back. A smile fluttered over his face and settled in his gentle blue eyes. He was a slim man, all in blue, even his socks. Myri calculated that her waist size would exceed his by least two inches. If he were a dog, he'd be a whippet, sleek and nervy.

Myri dug in but kept some restraint.

"I didn't make a total pig of myself," she said the next time Neil approached.

"Did you like it?" Neil asked while he bussed the dishes off the table and onto the tray and whisked away cracker crumbs.

"Yes. A little different than the way I make it." She hesitated.

"Yes, and that is how?" A booming voice came from behind. She swiveled in her chair. The man was well over six feet, round in the middle, dressed in a chef's cap and apron. The white apron had lost its starch and purity.

"The last time I made it, I used potato broth and crab broth and no milk." She wiped her mouth carefully and re-folded the napkin. She laid it on the table, grateful that she'd eaten before she saw the brown and red speckled apron.

"Humph." He belched. Small black beady eyes surveyed her with curiosity. If Neil was a whippet then Beans was a sloppy St. Bernard.

"This is Beans," Neil said with an adoring gleam in his eyes.

"Myri?" came a voice from the doorway.

All three of them turned.

"Rose, she's in here." Mrs. Dixon looked back over her shoulder. The woman who peeked from around Mrs. Dixon appeared to be in her early thirties, and definitely not in good health. Rose's sober gray eyes were weighted with baggy half circles. Her shoulder length auburn hair hung limp and lusterless.

"I'll be right there"— Myri searched the table for the bill. —"just as soon as I pay up."

"Neil handles the money," Beans said, squaring his shoulders and lifting his head. "I never use dairy in my chowders. Sometimes coconut milk," he added. The proclamation finished, he pivoted and went back into the kitchen.

Neil handed her the bill, which came to five dollars.

"You forgot the wine," Myri said.

"I didn't forget," he said, then lifted the tray of dirty dishes and glided away.

Myri put a ten dollar bill on the table.

CHAPTER TEN

The Dixon Story

I see you've met one of Seaview's oddest couples," Mrs. Dixon said when Myri joined them in the lobby. "And this is Mrs. Burton."

"We talked briefly on the phone," Myri said. "Glad to meet you."

"Call me Rose," the woman said, extending her hand. Her fingers were bony and cool. "Nice to put a face to the voice. Your hands are very warm on such a cold day."

Myri saw Mrs. Dixon's eyebrows inch up. Myri smiled and said nothing. She tipped her head, acknowledging Mrs. Dixon's response.

"The soup definitely warmed me up." Myri patted her stomach. "As did the wine. They were so nice. Didn't even charge me for the wine."

"That's like them," Rose said. She removed a khaki rain jacket and hung it on a coat rack near the front door. "They're so generous with their time and money. I think tonight's dinner is a fund raiser for the Humane Society."

"Let's sit over there." Mrs. Dixon pointed to an arrangement of chairs and a couch in a half circle near the fireplace.

"You're staying here?" Mrs. Dixon asked Myri.

"Yes, but I haven't checked in yet," Myri said. "When I called last week they had one room left at an off-season rate. The Pyramid Room. It's kind of funky, decorated in an Egyptian motif, an attic room. No private bath, but I can manage that."

"Excellent." Mrs. Dixon settled in one corner of the couch. Rose dropped into the other corner.

Myri sidled around a glass-topped coffee table heaped with maps, brochures and tide tables. An oval shallow bowl with an elongated glass float surrounded by sand dollars sat in the middle of the table. "I found one of these," Myri said, gently touching the watery blue float, "after a storm." She sank into an overstuffed gray and white striped chair. "This is an interesting place, but no internet or TV."

"Neil and Beans aren't fans of the communication revolution. They believe in getting away from it all," Mrs. Dixon said. "You'll eat and sleep well."

"I guess." Myri pulled out her cell. "No coverage." She turned the phone off and stuffed it back in her pocket.

"Coverage is good on the beach," Rose said.

A pause developed into a lengthy silence. Rose crossed her arms over her chest and stared at the fire. Myri followed her gaze. A gas log sent out an orange glow of safety and comfort. Outside the storm arrived. Except for the sound of the rain pelting the windows and the low hissing of the fire, all was quiet in an afternoon lull between lunch and dinner.

Myri picked up one of the sand dollars from the shallow bowl. She turned it over to study the delicate pattern. It fit nicely in the palm of her hand.

"Rose was a friend of my daughter's at college." Mrs. Dixon finally began. She kept her voice low and her tone steady.

"Rose's little girl, Susan, died last summer. She was going to be the flower girl in Karen's wedding but then, of course, all that changed."

"How did she die?" Myri asked.

"She was hit by a car. We aren't sure how it happened. It was so fast." Rose uncrossed her arms and picked fuzz off the ribbing around one of the cushions. "My son, Jimmy, was with her. He's eight this year. Susan was five. They were outside riding their bikes on the sidewalk." Her answer was memorized and toneless. "I went into the house to answer the phone. The driver said she fell into the road right in front of him."

Mrs. Dixon put her hand on Rose's shoulder.

"What did Jimmy say happened?" Myri asked.

"He says he didn't see what happened," Rose said. She reached for her purse on the floor and struggled with the zipper. She finally found a hankie, which she used to wipe her eyes and nose. "That's all he'll say. He clams up."

"Is he seeing a counselor or therapist?" Myri asked. "Are you?"

"My husband, he's the macho type, stiff upper lip, you know." Rose toyed with the crumpled hankie.

Myri knew the type. Macho men didn't impress her. She knew how to take care of herself, how to clean a bathroom as well as how to clean, load and shoot a shotgun. How to pluck a pheasant, gut it, and dig out the shot. Although the smell of fresh blood could be a little unsettling.

"I'm not a psychologist or anything," Myri said. "I don't know how I could help."

"There is a Buddhist monastery at the north end of the Peninsula, Way of Compassion." Mrs. Dixon searched for a map on the table. "Here, see near Ledbetter State Park." She spread the map out for Myri to see. "Every year they have a special ceremony, a Jizo ceremony for lost children. Everyone is welcome. We," Mrs. Dixon scooted close to Rose and put her arm around her shoulder, "were hoping you could go with us tomorrow. It's only two hours in the morning."

"I don't know anything about Buddhism." Myri leaned forward to gently settle the sand dollar back in its place.

"We don't either," Mrs. Dixon said, "but this ceremony is open to anyone. It doesn't matter what religion you are. It's very simple, almost all in silence. The family members make a small remembrance, like a necklace or a kerchief, and dedicate it to the lost child by decorating small statues called Jizos in the Jizo garden."

"Stan, my husband, thinks it's a silly waste of time," Rose said. She blushed. "But it's free and he thinks it'll stop my nagging."

"Rose, Stan and Jimmy made a kite. Susan loved the kite festival." Mrs. Dixon went on, "Tomorrow they plan to write some words on it and make a tail of Susan's hair ribbons."

"I haven't been able to throw the ribbons away," Rose said.

Myri drew in a deep breath. "I don't mind going, but I don't know how I can help."

"Don't worry about that. Just come. We'll pick you up at nine-thirty." Mrs. Dixon stood. "The program starts at ten tomorrow morning. Dress warm and casual. Some of it is outside."

Myri watched them bundle up to face the rain and wind. Once they were out the door, she went to the reception desk and tapped the bell. No one responded. She went back to the chair near the fire to wait. Check in time was at four.

After sorting through the brochures, she emptied the bowl of the sand dollars, studying each one before picking up the glass float. The float she'd found was round. Rolling pin styled ones, she'd heard, were rare. When she went to replace it, she noticed a design on the bowl. Two thirds of it was painted a marine blue. In the lower right corner, on a cliff looking out to sea, was a miniature shepherd with a flock of sheep. Myri carefully emptied the bowl and turned it over.

CHAPTER ELEVEN

Another Gilbert

The receptionist arrived at three fifty-five. She hurried up to the desk and dropped a bundle of menus on the counter.

"Hi," Myri said and waited for the woman to take off and shake a soggy raincoat. "I have a reservation: Myri Wolfen."

"Just give me a minute." She tugged down the cuffs of a fluffy white cardigan and adjusted a name tag identifying her as Teresa. "I have to get these"— she picked up the menus —"to the cook before he has a cow and I mean, a cow."

When she returned, her round face was red.

"Well, really!" She brushed a hank of brown hair away from her face. "He told me I looked like an overweight cream puff."

Myri stifled a smile. It was an apt description. Teresa was a tall, hefty woman. The long, beige empire-waist granny dress she wore billowed out from her hips as she walked. The fluffy sweater accentuated an ample torso.

"Maybe from a cook that's a compliment," Myri said.

"You know why they call him Beans?" She stopped, leaving Myri to draw her own conclusions. "Well, anyway, he said to give this to you." She held out what looked like a bookmark. "He called you the weird broad with spiky hair and muskrat eyes."

"I've been called worse." Myri shrugged. "What is it?"

"It's a ticket for the dinner tonight. He said you could pay what you could afford. It starts at six."

"That's nice of him."

"Nice. I think not," huffed the overweight cream puff.

"And now about checking in," Myri said.

"Since we had a cancellation this morning, I suppose I could give you the Jane Austen room, Number 6, for ten dollars more." Teresa tapped away at a computer under the counter.

"Thanks, but the Pyramid Room is fine. Sounds interesting."

"I guess, if you like pictures of mummies and weird half-human, half-animal gods. It's not Christian."

Myri kept silent. The Pyramid Room probably wasn't the only thing Teresa disapproved of.

"Up the stairs"— Teresa pointed to a side hall between the reception area and the bar —"in the back. Bathroom is on the second floor. "

"Great." Myri accepted the key. "And now could you tell me where that bowl came from?" She pointed to the coffee table.

"Neil brought it in last week. He bought it from some strange guy at the Saturday market." The phone rang. "Claiborne Inn, Teresa speaking."

Later, during the dinner, Myri asked Neil for information. He'd bought the dish at the local farmer's market from a man selling ceramics. He remembered the vendor had a buzz cut, wore a black tunic and black cotton pants. She was lucky to get any information from Neil as he fluttered back and forth between the dining room and the kitchen, kept the wine flowing, the dinner on schedule and Beans under control.

CHAPTER TWELVE

The Jackal God

The next morning she skipped breakfast. "I'm still totally full," she said to Mrs. Dixon. "It was lovely." Myri sighed. "A true French country meal: an aperitif, crusty bread, pâté, endive salad, cassoulet, a cheese tray and brandy."

"Stop," Mrs. Dixon said. "I barely got a piece of toast this morning."

Mrs. Dixon had arrived promptly at nine-thirty in a silver Mercedes. Rose was in the front passenger seat.

"Made me have wild dreams though," Myri said, "too much food and wine or maybe the wallpaper of hieroglyphics and strange beasts, half-man, half-wolf."

"The Jackal God, Anubis." Rose twisted around to speak directly to Myri. "The spirit guide that weighs the heart to decide if the dead get into eternity." Her eyes came to life. "I was an archaeology major."

"Thanks, but I like my spirit guides more friendly looking," Myri said, a remark that made Rose frown.

"Stan and Jimmy are meeting us there," Rose said. "Stan wanted to get a couple of things for the kite."

They followed a narrow road north and Seaview merged into Long Beach without any particular announcement or warning. Myri saw more "Closed for Winter" signs and enough "Gone out of Business" signs to be impressed that the Claiborne was still a viable business.

Eight miles after leaving Long Beach, they came to a four way stop. A secondhand bookstore on the Pacific side was closed, as was the Ice Cream Emporium across from it, but Jake's Mercantile on the east side was bubbling with Sunday business.

"This is a good spot for your cell if you need to use it," Rose said.

"Maybe I will just check in," Myri said. Mrs. Dixon pulled into the Mercantile's parking lot.

"I'm going to get a cup of coffee. Anyone else?" Mrs. Dixon asked.

"I'm fine," Rose said.

"No thanks," Myri said. "Good reception here. Four bars." There was one message from her neighbor, LuAnn, Zoe's owner.

"Myri, when you get this, give me a call. I had to call the cops to your place last night. Zoe went bananas about eleven and, when I let her out, she raced towards your place. I could see a light around the shop, so I called Greg Perez. You know, the cop at the end of our road. Everything is fine. I think Zoe scared whoever was there away, but I know Greg wants to talk with you."

Myri erased the message and then hit the call button. No answer.

"Hey, this is Myri. I'll have the phone off for a couple of hours. I am coming home today, but late. Thanks."

"Everything okay?" Rose swiveled around.

"Yes, I think so," Myri said.

"All ready?" Mrs. Dixon opened the car door and settled the cup into the holder next to her.

Five miles later, a cropping of beach homes and campsites announced the end of the paved road.

"Did you grow up here?" Myri asked.

"No, I met Stan at WSU, actually on a dig near Palouse Falls. He was in Anthropology. He wanted to come back to his hometown. He had great hopes of opening a bicycle shop. You might have seen it as you came into Seaview, near the Tourist Information Center." Rose lowered the visor and adjusted it so she could see Myri in the mirror.

Except for the momentary spark when she was talking about Archaeology, Rose's gray eyes weren't any happier today than the day before, but they were different. They had changed color from gray to topaz, a response to the silky yellow raincoat she wore. It was belted at the waist. The smallness of the circle made Myri wince. Rose's too-slender frame bowed, and her shoulders hunched over as though she carried a heavy weight.

"But it didn't work out, the bicycle shop, I'm afraid," Rose said. "We didn't have enough cushion to weather the winter season and a recession."

"I noticed a lot of *closed* and *going out of business* signs," Myri said.

"Actually, the economic downturn is what drew the Monastery here," Mrs. Dixon said. She slowed the Mercedes to below twenty miles an hour as the road roughened. "They were able to buy Surfside Center for about half of what it was listed for two years ago. And it has been perfect for them. There's a big central lodge with a convention-size kitchen and a dining area downstairs, a ballroom they made into a zendo, dormitory style bedrooms upstairs, as well as several small guest cottages and lots of grounds."

"How do you know so much about them?" Myri scooted up close to the front seats. "What's a zendo?"

Mrs. Dixon didn't answer. She concentrated on crossing a one lane wooden bridge leading from the gravel road onto the Monastery grounds. A sign arched over the bridge read *Way of Compassion Zen Monastery*.

The next sign, a white arrow tagged with a bouquet of balloons, directed them to a grassy parking area.

As soon as Mrs. Dixon put the Mercedes in park, Rose opened the door.

"Stan and Jimmy are probably already here," she said.

Myri gathered her jacket and a hat and put them on before following Rose. The stormy weather of the day before had passed, leaving behind a patchy cloud cover with brief breaks of sunshine. She could hear the surf, but sand dunes covered with clumps of reedy straw colored grass obstructed the view.

"Mom." A boy bolted from one of the cars. Myri would have recognized him anywhere as

Rose's son. He had the same auburn hair, pancake-sized gray eyes and slim shoulders. The man who followed him was under six feet with curly black hair and brown eyes. Although he was thin, he had a broad chest. Myri couldn't find a canine description to classify him. She thought instead of an arrow in a drawn bow, taut and single-minded.

"Jimmy." The man dashed after him. "Watch out for cars."

The boy threw himself into Rose's waiting circle of arms.

"Shssh." Rose kissed the top of his head and then took his hand. "Remember we are supposed to be very quiet here." She kneeled in front of him and leaned in to whisper. "It's a special time and place." She rose up. "Did you find what we need for the kite?"

"Darn. It's in the trunk." Stan wheeled around, heading back to a white Toyota Camry with a bicycle rack on the back.

Myri struggled to zip up her jacket in the wind. Next to her, Rose pulled down the earflaps on Jimmy's cap before she bent to snap up his coat. The sun broke through the clutter of clouds, momentarily sending a shaft of sunshine on the three of them.

Myri finished with the zipper and studied the parking area. There were ten cars besides Mrs. Dixon's Mercedes. She saw several couples hiking up the hill to the main entrance of the lodge.

"We can follow the crowd," Myri said, turning back to Rose and Jimmy. She froze. Jimmy stood as if in a spotlight. Pulsating energy swirled around him. He was the eye of a tornado.

"What is it?" Mrs. Dixon tapped Myri's shoulder.

"I don't know," Myri said. First Johnny Valentine and now this eight-year-old.

Neither had energy coming from them. Neither was connected to the web of being.

"Something important?" Mrs. Dixon came alongside Myri.

"Maybe. I can't explain it." Myri shrugged.

"Let's go." Stan carried a diamond-shaped kite in one hand and a grocery sack in the other. "I bought some colored markers and some glitter."

"I have the ribbons." Rose held up a plastic sealed sandwich bag.

"And I brought some beads and wire to make Karen something," Mrs. Dixon said.

The sun went behind the clouds, once again leaving the day cold and gray. "What's meant to happen will happen." Mrs. Dixon scooped Myri's elbow in her hand. "Don't worry about it. You'll know the right thing to do. I'm sure of it. And Ruby is sure of it."

Myri stopped. She watched as Stan, Rose and Jimmy began the gentle climb to the Lodge. The top of the hill couldn't be much over sea level, but the second floor rooms were high enough to have an ocean view.

CHAPTER THIRTEEN

Jizo Ceremony

Two stout bald-headed nuns with smiling faces and smiling eyes stood at the front door directing traffic. Then came the registration table where everyone signed in, giving their name, their hometown, and the name of the child to be remembered. After that, each person was handed a program and a map of the facility and the grounds.

The monk handing out the maps was half again as tall as Myri. She dubbed him "stilts." Except for Stilts and the Abbess, who was dressed in traditional black robes with an overlay of saffron sash, the rest of the staff, male or female, were indistinguishable in the simplicity of their black cotton trousers, black tunics, shaved heads, and lowered eyes.

After an introduction and a welcome by the Abbess, the participants moved into the zendo for a brief meditation period. The traditional mats and cushions used in the meditation hall were stacked to one side. Two rows of chairs lined the path to the altar where a large bronze Buddha sat between two lit candles and incense holders. Following the meditation, the group was led to the dining hall, which was set up with a dozen eight-foot tables stocked with paintbrushes, crayons, scissors and rolls of butcher paper. A sewing machine was available, surrounded by an assortment of cloth squares.

The monks sat motionless at intervals around the room. When waved over for consultation, the conversation was kept private and hushed.

"Jimmy," Rose huddled close to him and whispered, "please sit still and help us with the kite."

Myri sat across from Jimmy and, when Mrs. Dixon offered her a tin of beads and some wire, she joined the others in making remembrances. Stan lounged at the head of the table, cleaning his fingernails with a small penknife. Rose pushed a red marker towards him. He pushed it back. Jimmy dropped his head and sat on his hands. He beat his heels against the floor. Rose pushed the marker back towards Stan and rolled her eyes toward Jimmy.

Stan snapped the knife shut, grabbed the marker and made a heart design on the kite's wings. Rose added several spots of glue and sprinkled glitter. Jimmy wiggled in his seat and refused a handful stars that Rose offered him.

Forty-five minutes later, Stilts struck a three-foot brass gong that hung next to the entrance to the zendo. Everyone stood and filed back into the zendo for the closing ceremony. As the name of each deceased child was read, family members approached the altar and left a picture. Next, a monk sitting on the floor near the altar beat a drum and intoned for a second time the name of each child. At the end of the roll call, a dedication of merit was made for the benefit of all sentient beings. Families and friends were then encouraged to wander the grounds to decorate the small Jizo statues or to engage in whatever devotional activity they deemed useful.

The Abbess stood at the door, stopping each person for a moment as she put her hands together and bowed to them. Stan, Rose, Jimmy, Mrs. Dixon, and Myri were the last group out, the last to be delayed. The Abbess made eye contact and bowed. Myri, in her turn, stared back. She was drawn into the Abbess's boundless hazel eyes.

No fooling her. The Abbess had an ancient soul with the endurance of a sea-going turtle. Myri bobbed her head, put her hands together and bowed back. A smile flickered over the Abbess's face. She reached out, covering Myri's hands with her own. Instead of heat, Myri felt a cool quieting of energy.

Once outside, families drifted off in different directions. Some studied the maps they'd been given. Others seemed to know where they wanted to go. The Monastery staff filtered out, divided themselves into small groups and followed. Myri spotted Mrs. Dixon on a path at the base of the hill that circled back into the Jizo garden. Stan, Jimmy and Rose were in the parking area, headed for the path through the sand dunes and onto the beach.

Myri hurried down the slope. Stan was in the lead and carried the kite; Rose and Jimmy trailed behind holding hands.

When Myri topped the dunes she saw the tide was out. The air was full of a fermented fishy smell arising from clumps of rubbery brown kelp that lay in tangled piles along the high water mark. There were a couple of beachcombers walking north towards the Ledbetter Light House that rose up in dark profile at the very end of the peninsula. A figure close by, at the base of the sand dune ridge, sauntered, stopping often to search the ground.

Stan ran into a southwesterly wind, letting out string. Rose and Jimmy watched as the kite climbed.

"Hey, Jimmy," Myri called out. "Let's catch him." She put out her hand and he took it. It was slow going in the dry, soft sand and they bobbled back and forth, but as soon as they hit the packed damp area, they picked up speed.

"Here, son," Stan yelled back. "Come and take her."

Jimmy stopped.

"Let me." Myri folded over, hands on her thighs, for a quick deep breath and then reached up for the spool. Stan handed it over to her and then drifted back towards Rose, leaving Myri and Jimmy side by side.

The kite bounced around in the sky with the ribbons trailing.

"You want to try getting it higher?" Myri held the spool out. He shook his head no.

"You're a good runner," Myri said. "I bet you could have done this all by yourself."

"No," he cried out. "I'm bad." He started to cry; his lips and chin quivered. "I'm a bad boy."

Myri glanced first up at the kite and then, assured that it was holding its own in the wind, shifted her gaze to Jimmy.

"No, you're not bad," Myri said. "You're just sad."

"I'm bad," he insisted and kicked up sand.

"No. No, you're not." A deep male voice came from behind them. Myri turned to see who it was, but by then the man had come around and sank to his knees in front of Jimmy. All Myri could identify was the black loose pants and tunic of one of the Monastery staff. His head wasn't shaved, but his black hair was cut marine style to within an inch. He put his arms around the boy and brought his face close to Jimmy's – almost nose to nose. "Maybe you did a bad thing, but you're not bad."

"I pushed her." Jimmy squinted his eyes, turned his face skyward and wailed.

"Give the kite to me." The man lifted his hand up, never taking his eyes off Jimmy face.

Myri brought the string within his reach. She tried to open her hand.

"My hand won't open," Myri gasped.

"Give it to him." The man pointed to Jimmy. "What's your name?"

When Jimmy didn't respond Myri answered. "His name's Jimmy." She lowered the spool.

Jimmy reached for it slowly.

"It was a mistake," the man said. "That's all. You can let go of a mistake. You can let go of the kite."

Jimmy dropped the spool to the ground; the kite jerked upward but held constant, anchored by the weight of the spool. The man dug a small penknife from his pocket and cut the string, but even then the kite stayed in place. The string dangled in front of Jimmy.

"I know something that might help." The man smoothed Jimmy's hair. "You can say I'm sorry. It was a mistake."

Jimmy glanced anxiously between the man's face and the kite.

"I'm sorry," Jimmy whispered. "It was a mistake."

"Hey, what's going on?" Stan rushed up to Myri. "Who's this?"

Rose came alongside. She was breathless, but grabbed Jimmy into the safety of her arms.

The man stood, staring upward.

The kite ascended. Finally, it sailed away in the wind.

Myri watched as it climbed. When she turned back, a cloud-shadow surged over the group, then just as quickly passed. Jimmy clung to Rose and stared up at the kite. Stan put his arm around

Rose's shoulder. The unknown man stood and concentrated on Jimmy. Myri kept her eyes unfocused and shifted her attention to the alternating patterns of darkness and light swirling around the Burton trio.

The energy field around Jimmy reconfigured. Pulsing strands of energy now ran through them, and father, mother, son were linked together as in a jeweled web.

At that moment the unknown man became known to Myri. He was taller by six inches, broader at the shoulder, slimmer at the waist, with a long torso and short legs, an ancient Mayan in physique, but the eyes were the same. Michael Gilbert.

CHAPTER FOURTEEN

Alive

W ho are you?" Stan studied Michael. "Are you from the Monastery? You're dressed like them."

"I'm Michael Gilbert and, yes, I'm staying at the Monastery for a while. I was searching for beach glass when I saw this boy needed some help with the kite."

"This is Jimmy's dad, Stan, and his mom, Rose," Myri said.

"Are you here for the Jizo ceremony?" Gilbert asked.

"Yes." Rose straightened the collar on Jimmy's coat. "The kite was for our daughter, Jimmy's little sister, who died last summer."

"Oh." Gilbert nodded. "I think I see. I'm a big brother, too." He kneeled down again in front of Jimmy. "Sometimes, there is nothing we can do, except to say we're sorry and to let go."

Jimmy's gray eyes glistened. He rubbed a coat sleeve under his nose.

"MYRI," Mrs. Dixon shouted as she came toward them waving her hand back and forth.

"Your phone was ringing when I got back to the car and I answered it. Here." She shoved it towards Myri. "It was a policeman... Perez. He said you need to call him back."

"It's time we all go back," Stan said, putting out his hands – one each to Rose and Jimmy. He leaned back his head and searched the sky. The kite had disappeared.

Myri took the phone and hit the redial button. She trailed along slowly, holding the phone to her ear.

Gilbert waited for her at the top of the dune.

"No bars all of a sudden." She swung the cell in the air, trying to locate a good reception area. "Somebody tried to break into my place last night. I need to get home."

"Where's home?" he asked. He reached out to steady her down the last steps of the slope.

"The east side. Tri-Cities."

"You're kidding me." He grinned. "I grew up in Pasco."

"Yeah, small world."

"Hey"— he stopped and frowned— "if it's not too much to ask, this would be a good opportunity for me to get a ride home. I've been promising Mom. I could catch a bus back from Pasco.

Myri shrugged. "Sure."

"Wait here." He motioned for her to stay. "Wait right here. I won't be long. I have to tell Cho Y."

"Who is that?" Mrs. Dixon rested against the Mercedes. She jutted her chin at Gilbert's back.

"His name is Michael Gilbert. Do you mind if he rides back to town with us?" Myri leaned against the car beside Mrs. Dixon. "He helped Jimmy with the kite."

"He helped Jimmy with the kite," Mrs. Dixon repeated. She stared into Myri's face.

Myri bobbed her head. Mrs. Dixon pushed away from the car and walked over to say good-bye to Rose. They hugged and then, arm-in-arm, they came toward Myri.

"Thanks. Something is different." Rose stretched her hand toward Myri. "What happened? We were too far away to hear."

Before Myri could respond, Michael hurried up to them, carrying a green canvas sports bag. The Abbess churned up the hem of her black robes in an effort to keep up with him.

"Lunch is at noon." The Abbess came to a stop. She held her hands cupped lightly at waist level. "You'd all be welcome."

"We need to get home," Rose said. "But thanks so much for everything." She included all of them in the expanse of her gratitude.

After the family got in the car, the Abbess invited Mrs. Dixon and Myri again to stay for lunch.

"If Mrs. Dixon doesn't mind, I need to go," Myri said. "It's a long drive home."

"Thanks for helping," the Abbess said. "I see the boy is better." The Abbess waved to Jimmy whose face was pushed to the glass in the back seat window. He waved back as the car passed.

"You see he's better?" Myri tilted her head closer to the saffron-robed shoulder.

"I see his heart is now open, full of energy. And, yes, better – alive."

Alive. Maybe that explained Valentine. No energy field without a heart, not really alive. No compassion or humanity.

The Abbess's gentle sigh and instruction to Michael interrupted her thoughts.

"Michael," Cho Y said, facing him, "we'll hear from you soon. Hozen can come get you in Portland. Be mindful."

It was an odd thing to say: *be mindful.*

CHAPTER FIFTEEN

Return

There aren't many places to stop between here and Longview and after we leave Interstate 5, even fewer," Myri said.

The Honda Civic seemed smaller when Michael got in. He scooted the seat back as far as it would go, but nothing could be done about the bulk of his shoulders which filled up not only his space but encroached on the space between the front seats divided by the gear box.

"I'm good," he said. He fiddled with the seat back, adjusting the lever on the side so he reclined. "At the Monastery the bell rings every morning at 3:55 a.m. Hope you don't mind if I nod off for a while." He folded his arms and sank back against the seat.

Myri checked the dashboard clock. With luck they could be back in the Tri-Cities by seven. The radio boomed when she started the engine.

"Jazz, something we don't get in the Tri-Cities." She turned the volume down.

"Not a problem," he yawned, "poke me in the ribs if I start to snore. They put me in one of the guest rooms at the Monastery. Cho Y was kind about it, but firm. Her monks and nuns needed their sleep."

"So you're not a monk?" Myri asked.

"No. For room and board I agreed to spend about six months helping them with an art project. One of the stipulations was that I follow their schedule." He closed his eyes. "I'm not sure which is tougher, boot camp or monk camp."

Between the mellow Sunday jazz program, the mist, the trees, and the highway devoid of logging trucks, Myri enjoyed the ensuing silence as Michael settled into a rhythmic breathing pattern.

He didn't stir until she slowed down in Stevenson – about an hour east after leaving the Interstate 5 and exiting onto Washington state Highway 12 where it paralleled the Columbia River.

"We're about three hours from home," she said. "I need a pit stop and something to eat.

There's a little Mexican place that has good tamales."

He levered the seat forward to sit up. "Sounds great to me."

She turned right at the first light and slowed for pedestrians. At the end of the block, she pulled to the curb, but the window at La Bonita was dark. *Closed on Sundays* the sign in the door read.

"Okay, next best option is probably the Safeway deli." She flicked on the turn signal to re-enter the traffic.

"Nothing could come close to my momma's tamales anyway," he said.

"I'm always on the lookout for a good tamale," she said. "I'm a first class foodie."

"In that case, I'll make sure you get some homemade ones from mi casa." He reached in the back to retrieve the sports bag and extracted a wallet.

"I'll buy dinner," he said, "and give you some gas money."

A Sunday afternoon lull had settled on the grocery store. There were few shoppers. At the deli counter they had to ring for service. The warming trays of Chinese food, mixed stir veggies, Kung Pao Chicken, and fried rice were half-empty and crusted with brown sauce.

"Half a roast beef," Myri ordered. "Everything on it." Michael went with the veggie delight, tomato with avocado and Swiss cheese.

He handed her a ten after paying for sandwiches and drinks. Michael ate quickly and finished first. "Sorry," he chuckled. "At the monastery we eat ritual oryoki-style. One bowl, no conversation, no fuss."

Myri shrugged. "Not a problem. The sooner we're on the road the better."

After clearing the table of the paper and napkins, they both headed for the restrooms in the back.

"Next stop: the Tri-Cities," she said as they climbed back in the car, and she released the brake.

"I've never been down the Washington side." He buckled up. "We always go the freeway from Portland."

"I hate freeways," Myri said. "This way through the gorge you can see the changes from forest to desert. It's too early for the wild flowers, but about April, the lupine and the black-eyed daisies are everywhere."

"No phone reception." He snapped his cell shut.

"No, or radio from here on." She bumped his shoulder in opening the storage console. "But I have some CDs."

"Norah Jones, and Linda Ronstadt's 'Canciones de mi Padre,' nice." He flipped the holder open. "You speak Spanish?"

Myri laughed. "Dos cervezas. That's it."

He fed the disc player both albums.

"You seem familiar to me." He adjusted the seat back.

"Middle school, Stevens in Pasco. You were ahead of me."

"Really? That's a long time ago."

"I remember you. I remember eyes."

"I wasn't there long."

"No, you weren't."

"I was twelve, thirteen when I started picking asparagus." He adjusted the volume up. "Small world."

Driving demanded Myri's attention. The two-lane road snaked and switched back and forth, climbing the grade that topped out near Dog Mountain trailhead. The descent into the gorge brought changes in the landscape. The pine trees gradually gave way to a ragged forest of scrub oak that dwindled into fields of stubby sagebrush.

"See that?" Myri pointed to outcroppings of ancient lava that rose in spindles from the earth. "Makes me think of ghosts or gods rising from the earth."

"I'd like to get a picture of it, if you wouldn't mind stopping." He reached into the back seat. "I don't go anyplace without my camera."

Myri slowed and pulled to the side of the road. Two motorcycles, side by side, roared past them.

"There's a little sun left," Myri said.

She watched Michael navigate the gravelly slope from the road to a set of railroad tracks. Once over the tracks, he was held back by a barbed wire fence. He retreated from the fence and kneeled down, taking several shots. About a hundred yards south he snapped several more before returning to the car.

"Interesting stuff," he said.

"Can I see?" Myri craned her head over his shoulder.

He leaned over to show her. "Black and white might be more impressive."

"Is that what you're helping with at Way of Compassion, photography?" Myri asked after he clicked through the photos. She checked the rearview mirror and let a pick-up pulling a ski-boat go by.

"Is that right?" Michael pointed to a sign. "No services for the next sixty miles."

Myri boosted the speed to sixty-five and then punched in the cruise control. "Nothing except wide open space and a few critters."

After he wiped the camera and replaced the lens cover, he placed it on the back seat.

"No, to your question. I'm helping them set up production of the Jizo statues so that they can sell them on line. Photography is a passion, but working with ceramics and glass is what I do best."

"Like the plates?"

"You know about them?"

"A little."

"Hey." He reached for the volume control. "Here's your song. For the lady who notices eyes."

Linda Ronstadt's voice came slow and plaintive.

"*There are some eyes*," he translated. He sang the chorus in Spanish. Myri caught one or two of the words. He finished in a soft, mournful sigh. She caught the gist of it.

"Giving your life for someone else? Not for me. I'm not a romantic," she said.

The sun dipped below the edge of the canyon, leaving the sky in shades of purple. Myri scanned the road, staying alert, watching for deer that often moved at dusk.

He gave her a gentle jab in the ribs. "Come on. Don't I see a sparkle in those black eyes of yours? There must be someone."

She turned the volume louder. Revealing herself didn't usually pan out. It wasn't only her dad who didn't want to deal with weirdness.

CHAPTER SIXTEEN

Wrong Way

Is this road on the map?" Michael asked. There was no moon, no city lights and no traffic. Stars filled the crystal clear sky. They sped along in a silent, dark world, scouted by the Civics' headlights.

"It's a back road into Kennewick, over the Horse Heaven Hills," Myri said. "We're only thirty-nine miles away."

"How did you know it was here?"

"My dad. He was a trucker, and truckers know back roads and how to avoid weigh stations when they need to."

"He sounds interesting."

"Was. He died last year."

"I'm sorry. Your mom? Have any brothers and sisters?"

"No brothers or sisters and my mom died when I was three."

"Rough. I have four sisters and three brothers. There's always something going on, some drama or other."

When she slowed to make a right onto Clodfelter, he pushed forward, studying the road.

"It's like we're in the middle of nowhere. There's no sign to Kennewick, nothing."

Myri tapped the odometer. "Exactly thirteen miles from Highway 12. That's how I know."

"I guess you can find your way to my place then. It's off Badger Mountain Road. My family owns the junk yard."

"Sure, I know it. My dad loved trucks, cars, anything with an engine and wheels. As a kid I spent a lot of time waiting while he wandered around hunting for parts. But I thought old man Redding owned that place."

"My dad and brothers bought it a few years back. They fixed up the shop so my two younger brothers could live there."

"Hold on, this is the fun part, like a roller coaster." Myri gunned the engine over one hill, dropping quickly on the other side into a gully. At the bottom, another steep grade appeared and she hit the gas.

Michael braced himself, both hands on the glove box.

At the top she braked for a sharp right turn. The valley below was dotted with lights.

"Home," Myri said.

"None too soon. I hurl easy."

"Not me. A cast iron stomach."

"Habaneros?" Michael asked.

"You got me there. They're way too hot for me."

At the bottom of the grade, Badger Mountain Road intersected Clodfelter, and Myri edged to the left to make the turn west. Before she could turn, she heard a tornado of sirens. She scanned the roads in every direction. When the sound intensified, Myri quickly pulled to the right edge to wait. Flashing lights came from the east. A fire engine and a police car slowed for the intersection, but once through barreled down the road.

She had just made the turn east when another police car raced up behind her with its siren wailing and its lights flashing. She immediately pulled to the side. Behind the police car was an ambulance in full throttle and full flashing lights, alarm screeching.

"What the –?" Michael sat up. "They're at the junk yard."

Double gates in the eight-foot chain link fence were thrown back and three police cars barricaded the entrance. The ambulance worked around the barricade and rocked to a stop at a side entrance to a large metal building. Two policemen were at the door directing the medics.

Myri slowly pulled the Civic up to the police cars. Michael shoved the door open at the same time he struggled to unfasten the seat belt.

"Hey, buddy, slow down." An officer approached the car.

"My God, what's happening? Where are my brothers?" Michael lunged forward.

"I'm telling you. Stay where you are." The officer moved into a wide stance and shook his finger at Michael.

Myri cut the engine and got out.

"This is his folks' place." Myri inched up to stand beside Michael. "We just got into town."

"Okay. But stay where you are. People in there are hurt and you can't help them. They"— the officer pointed to the ambulance —"can help them."

"Got it. Got it." Michael crossed his arms over his chest. "We'll stay put."

The officer backed away, holding up his hand as a stop sign.

Myri and Michael could see into the gap between the police cars. Two bodies were on the ground.

The medics came out of the side door wheeling a gurney.

"I can't tell who it is from here," Michael said.

Myri inched forward to peer over the hood of the police car. In the rotating red and white strobe glare, she saw Ruby and Samson. They were standing next to the two bodies on the ground, but neither was focused on the area at their feet. They were focused on something behind Myri.

Myri turned to follow their gaze. On the other side of the road, there was a boarded up mini-mart. Along the side of the building in the shadows, the red and white flashing lights bounced off a silver Lincoln town car. If Johnny Valentine was here, where was Al?

She knew with a moment's reflection where Al was. She closed her eyes and swallowed, then turned around to face the area in front of Ruby and Samson. She opened her eyes slowly, scanning the ground near the bodies first. There it was—the Mariners' stocking hat.

The smell of blood made her knees weak and she slumped against the police car.

"Myri!" Michael rushed forward to soften her crash to the ground.

"I'm okay." She waved him away. She bent over, head down and breathed deeply. "I'm an almost fainter."

A police officer came over to the car. He wore a brown uniform of the Sheriff's department.

"Myri, what are you doing here?"

"Greg. What's going on?"

Officer Greg Perez clamped his jaws together and swung his head back and forth.

"Nasty business. The other officer told me you were family?" Perez glared at Michael. "What's your name? Let me see some ID."

"It's in the car." While Michael retrieved his green bag from the back seat, Myri explained the situation.

"Myri, you go home. I'll call you tomorrow. And you, Mr. Gilbert, come with me. Perhaps you can help us."

"Michael, call me. I'm in the book."

Myri backed out into the road. The headlights from the Civic lit up the clothing on the bodies. One was dressed in black and white striped overalls but neither of them had on a brown cashmere coat or brown tasseled loafers.

She glanced left. The Lincoln was gone.

CHAPTER SEVENTEEN

Waiting

Myri made a tangled mess of the sheets, twisting and turning all night long, falling asleep two hours before the alarm went off. The morning was rainy and gray. She wasn't hungry for breakfast, and neither the usual aroma of coffee nor the first sip lightened her spirits. Even her hands were on vacation. A snowball would have remained solidly compact in them. She made it to work on time and put in a half day in Sol's domain at the back of the hardware store tidying boxes of oil filters.

Neither Greg nor Michael called. The only source of information was the front page of the *Mid-Columbia Herald*. The black and white picture made the junk yard surrounded by the fence look like a prison. Three men and two dogs died on the scene. A fourth man died on the way to the hospital.

Another Drug Deal Gone Bad was the *Herald* headline. There was an insinuation the junkyard shop was a pivotal point of drug running, a place where cars were chopped to make special hidey holes.

Two of the dead men on the scene were Gilberts, Seth, 21 and Tony, 19. Al Bates was the third. The fourth's name was being held pending notification of the family.

Myri was sure both Greg and Michael would call. Michael because his camera sat on her kitchen table. He had not re-stowed it, and in his hurry to fetch his bag for ID had left it behind on the back seat. Greg would call to follow up on the attempted break-in of her shop.

There was nothing to be done except to wait, wait for the calls, wait for the obits, wait for the funeral announcements.

Myri went outside in the garden. The clouds had broken; the rain abated. A weak pale sun made a feeble attempt to warm the damp earth. She searched for any sign that the garden grew, but there were no green shoots in any of the rows. She paused to listen to the crows and heard the first raspy call of a male pheasant. She scanned the field next to the shop hoping to see him as he pranced his red breast across the open space. Instead, a smoky gray cat dashed from behind the shop, which sent the crows into a frenzy of cawing. The pheasant, flushed from hiding under a scrubby bit of sage, took flight.

CHAPTER EIGHTEEN

Nothing Missing

Tuesday came and there was still no call from either Greg or Michael. Death notices for both Gilbert boys and Al Baker were in the paper, but there was little else about the crime scene or suspects, although the police mentioned they were looking for a "person of interest."

Myri slept in the recliner in front of the TV. After a full day at the winery packaging wine club member shipments, she had nodded off. The newspaper lay open in her lap.

A knock on the door startled her. It was almost seven. She'd missed the local news.

"Myri, are you in there?" There was another knock, this one harder than the first.

"Just a minute." She rocked forward out of the chair. "Greg, come in." She yawned widely and rubbed her eyes.

"Sorry I didn't get to you yesterday," Greg said. He was poster perfect in his brown uniform. The trousers were perfectly pressed with a stiff center ridge down each leg. The peaked hat he removed so he could get through the door without ducking. He dangled it in his hands. "Have you had a chance to look over the shop? I couldn't see anything wrong." His steady hazel eyes made quick sweep of the living room. "Nothing wrong in here?"

"Nothing obvious."

"Let's go check it out together."

"We can go out the back," Myri said. She grabbed a set of keys from a key board next to the front door and then motioned for him to follow her down the hallway past the kitchen. "It's a muddy mess out there. Not real good for those shiny shoes of yours."

"I'll manage."

Myri unlocked the south facing shop door and flicked on the fluorescent lighting. To shed more light on the surrounding outside area, she hit the opener that lifted the broad garage door.

A green pickup truck was parked inside near the door. A three-foot wide work table ran the entire length on the other side. It was a jumble of wire, wrenches, cartons of washers and nuts, irrigation pipe and sprinkler heads. Shelving on the rear wall held empty canning jars. A compressor and a pressure washer were shoved under the shelving.

"Not much of value in here except the tools," Myri said and followed Greg. He opened the pickup's driver door and scanned the front seat.

"Dad had an extra storage compartment put under the back seat."

Greg folded the front seat forward. He lifted the cushion on the back seat to open the compartment.

"Chains, tools and a silver tackle box."

"Sounds about right."

"Where's the gun?" Greg shut the lid and replaced the cushion. "All of these old geezers carry a gun in their truck."

"Under the front seat." Myri went around to the passenger side and got in. She rummaged around under the seat until she felt the barrel. "It's loaded, so stand aside," she said. "Dad didn't have much use for an empty gun."

Greg came around to her side. She handed the rifle to him stock first, barrel down.

He checked the safety, tweaked the shell latch, and then pumped the action bar to eject the bullets.

"You see anything out of order in here?"

Myri made a three sixty turn. "I don't think anybody's been in here," she said. "The door hasn't been jimmied. The lock wasn't damaged."

"That dog must have scared him away." Greg walked closer to the workbench, scanning the surface.

"Speaking of the devil." Myri said.

Zoe sped like a torpedo through the garage opening. Her nails clicked over the cement. Myri kneeled down to keep from being bowled over.

"You devil." Myri grabbed the dog on both sides under her ears and scratched hard.

"That's more like a wolf than a dog." Greg came over. "Scary ice blue eyes."

"She's Siberian Husky." Myri continued scratching and Zoe nuzzled her chest.

"Likes you all right," Greg said.

"She likes the steak bones I save for her."

Zoe raised her head and gave Myri a lick on the mouth.

"That is disgusting." Greg gagged.

"Her mouth is cleaner than yours," Myri said.

"It's not surprising you don't have a boyfriend with that attitude. Rather kiss a dog."

"You jealous?" Myri grinned up at Greg.

"You had your chance." Greg stood taller and puffed up his chest. "I guess you haven't heard me and Ruthie Townsend are getting married in June."

"That blonde Barbie Doll? Fat chance I ever had. You were always a sucker for blondes and redheads," Myri pushed herself up.

"You jealous?"

"No." Myri said with a laugh, "You're way too high maintenance for me. It'll take a Ruthie to keep you in line."

"Probably." The thought brought a sly smile to his face.

"So tell me about the Gilberts," Myri said. "How are they doing? When's the funeral? Anything new on the situation?"

"Nothing new that isn't in the paper." Greg followed Myri to the front door where she hit the garage door button. The panel started a slow grinding descent that spooked Zoe. She raced outside. "The funeral's next Saturday at the Spirit of the Lamb in Pasco. You going?"

Myri pulled the door shut. "I'm going to the funeral but not to the reception afterwards. I've got to work a dinner at the winery."

Together they started back to the house.

Myri broke the short silence. "You know that guy got killed? Al Bates. He was out here with some dude from the Midwest, Johnny Valentine, a couple of weeks ago. Valentine seemed very interested in my dad's truck."

"Bates was the guy with part of his ear gone. He must have been a boxer. We don't know much about him, but we know plenty about Johnny, except where he is at the moment." He offered her the bullets that he'd been rolling around in his hand. "He's one mean son of a bitch. If he comes calling again, dial 911 as fast as you can."

Myri accepted the bullets. They lay cold and solid in her hand.

"Will do," she answered.

CHAPTER NINETEEN

Rest in Peace

On Saturday Myri arrived at Spirit of the Lamb so late that the all the pews were full. Extra chairs were placed in the alcove. Two flower laden caskets had already been wheeled down to the altar. Since she knew little of the liturgy and ritual, she sat through the bells, the candles, the swinging censors, the organ bass hum, and the prayers in silence. She alternated between standing and sitting as those around her rose and sat. After the final benediction, ushers soft soled it down two separate aisles to escort the family out. In the alcove, chairs were quickly vacated and stacked so the family could arrange a receiving line.

As soon as the line had formed, Myri queued up. Michael stood half way through the line. Myri identified herself as a "friend of Michael's", taking each hand in turn as it was offered. The glistening dark eyes of the women, the long, sad faces of the men reminded her of her own painful loss. She felt a tightness in her throat and her hands warmed up as she approached Michael.

"Myri, how nice of you to come." Michael hugged her.

"I'm so sorry," she said. She kept her head lightly against the hollow of his neck until she felt him pull away.

"Are you staying for dinner?" He left his hand on her shoulder. "It's here downstairs after the interment, about six."

"No. I've got to go to work, but I have your camera in the car. Do you want me to go get it?"

"I'll come." He stepped out of line and followed her outside. "You'd think by now the weather would warm up."

"It's the wind, makes everything seem colder." Myri pointed to an office parking lot across from the Church. "I'm over there."

They hurried across the street.

"When are you leaving?" Myri asked.

"Tomorrow. I can't stay here." He slung the camera over his shoulder. "It's too complicated. I need a quiet place to work. Thanks for coming."

"Here's my address and phone number." Myri handed him a folded piece of paper. "When you're next in town, call me. I still want some of your mama's tamales."

"I'll do what I can." He stepped back and offered his hand.

"Me too."

"Michael, Michael, Momma wants you."

"One of your sisters?" Myri asked. "She's so pretty. That long black braid reminds me of my mother."

"That's Liz, the youngest. She's taking it the hardest. She's still living at home."

Myri watched him dash across the street and rearrange a black lace shawl over his sister's shoulder before turning to wave.

CHAPTER TWENTY

Anubis

Later at the winery, Myri stacked the last saucers on the counter next to the dishwasher.

"Chris, I'm outta here." She untied the black apron and tossed it into the dirty clothes bag at the end of the counter.

"Go. Thanks for staying late." Chris rubbed his forehead. "The twins can finish up. And be careful. Wind warnings are in effect until tomorrow morning."

Myri paused just outside the winery doors and looked up at the sky. It was a moonless night. Sirius, the Dog Star, glittered brightly. She massaged her shoulders, leaning her head back. If that didn't help the kink in her neck she knew what would – a good stiff brandy.

As soon as she got home, she kicked off her shoes, went to the liquor cabinet, squatted in front of it and searched for the Delamain and a brandy snifter.

"Cheers," she toasted herself in the mirror over the cabinet. "Here's to spring."

Another reflection in the mirror made her spin around. The lights were on in the shop. She tried to remember if she had left them on. She scanned the driveway leading past the garden to the back. There were no cars parked in the driveway and none that she could see in the back lot. From the keys board she selected the shop keys, retrieved her cell from the dining room table then slipped on her shoes.

Before she tried the shop key she put her ear to the door. A gust of wind rattled a loose sheet of metal but she heard nothing else. With a gentle twist she rotated the knob and pushed. The door opened. There was a musky smell, a man's cologne. She stepped inside. The wind caught the door, slammed it violently before she could stop it.

The pickup's driver side door was open. She couldn't see the face, but she knew who it was by the tasseled loafers. Johnny Valentine was bent over the back seat of the pick-up with the chest open. The tackle box sat near his feet. He raised his head at the sound of the banging door.

He had a pistol in his hand. "I warned you." He pulled the trigger.

The cell she carried never made it to her ear. It bounced as it hit the floor.

She spun around. Searing pain gripped her, knees buckled. She thudded to the floor. Her cheek pressed against the frigid cement. The cold spread through her, followed by a wave of heat. Her whole body shimmied and then she lay quiet, hearing a high wire hum first then an eerie, echoing one word an acapella chant, OM. She had never felt so warm, so safe, so free, buoyed in a huge iridescent bubble, weightless, a floating prism of colorful refracted light. It was bliss, sheer bliss.

"Myri." Ruby emerged from the wall, her long black hair flowing behind her as if she was facing a stiff wind. The red caftan danced and fluttered like a cloud of butterflies.

"Ruby. This is wonderful."

"Myri, you can't stay." Ruby shimmered in front of her. "You have to go back."

"Back? Back where?" Myri followed Ruby's pointed finger.

Myri saw herself on the shop floor, a puddle of blood forming under her cheek.

"You have work to do."

"Myri, you in there?"

"Who's that?" Myri asked.

"It's Michael." Ruby's eyes became streaks of lighting. "You must go back and help him."

"I don't want to go back. I feel wonderful right here, besides there's nothing I can do. Johnny has a gun."

"You have what you need. You have your heart and your hands." Ruby pointed again with impatience."

Myri's lowered her eyes. "But you're here. It's too late."

"It's not too late." Ruby said. "But you must hurry. Decide now."

"Why?" Tears streamed down Myri's face. "I don't want to go. I'm scared."

"You must try," Ruby said softly, "not only for Michael but for yourself."

Myri wiped the tears from her eyes. If she couldn't trust Ruby who could she trust? She nodded sadly and immediately felt herself sucked down, her body getting denser and denser, more solid. She hurt. She was on the floor. Her hands were cold.

Johnny Valentine squatted behind the pickup door. He rolled the window down, and waited with the muzzle of the pistol resting on the window's edge. He sighted along the barrel.

Myri concentrated. Michael wouldn't stand a chance. He'd see her on the floor, come to her, oblivious to all else. Valentine already had a bead on him. Her hands began to warm. They throbbed. I must try. Ruby said I must try. She pushed up hard, stumbled, regained balance and flung herself in front of Michael. She closed her eyes and raised both hands fingers splayed. A field of energy vibrated in front of her. A shot rattled through the building. She felt her hands burn as the bullet struck the energized zone. The bullet ricocheted, bounced off the metal wall and struck Valentine. He looked surprised, put out a hand to brace himself against the pickup and then sank to the floor.

"My god, Myri. What is going on?" Michael stood rooted in confusion.

"I'm not sure." Myri felt her knees go watery. "It's not safe." She reached out to steady herself. "I don't feel so good." She backed up to the wall and slid to the floor. "What is that scratching noise?"

"It's the dog," Michael said. "When I drove up to your house, this dog ran up barking. It scared me. I thought it was after me, but it kept running and barking. And when you didn't answer the door, I came out here and it was scratching and whining to get in here."

"Zoe." Myri blinked. "It's Zoe."

"I didn't let her in," Michael said.

The door burst open and Zoe came in snarling. She brushed up against Myri and halted and then she stretched out beside her. Slowly Zoe rolled to one side and then over on her back.

"Why is she doing that?" Michael came closer.

"Michael, get out of here." Myri tried to get up.

"Your hands are all bloody." Michael bent down, and cupped her hands in his. "See."

"Michael!" Myri screamed. "Get out of here, now. Do as I tell you." Myri flung her arm towards the door. "Now."

Michael backed up, alarmed at her anger, staring at her.

"That man is hurt." Michael said.

"That man is not hurt. That man is dead. Now go."

"I can't leave you here, alone."

"Out. Zoe's here with me. Call 911."

Once he was outside, Myri pushed away from the wall and inched towards Zoe. "I see it too Zoe. It's alright." A spirit had arrived for

Johnny Valentine. It was not Ruby. Anubis had come, half man, half jackal.

Myri bent and gently stroked Zoe's stomach.

"Let's go," she whispered. "I know you don't understand, but we don't want to be here when Anubis weighs Valentine's heart. Up."

Myri tugged Zoe's collar. The dog whined but came to her feet. Slowly, both woman and dog backed out of the building.

"Do you hear that?" Myri put her hands over her ears. A savage, chilling scream blasted through the building.

"You mean the ambulance?" Michael checked Myri's face.

She sat down on the ground. "I think I'll faint now."

"You're an almost fainter, remember." Michael knelt in front of her.

"Sometimes I'm wrong."

CHAPTER TWENTY-ONE

Worth Its Weight

When she came to, both Greg and LuAnn were bent over staring her in the face. The strobe effect from the rotating lights on two police cars made her dizzy

"What happened?" Greg asked. His voice rose. "There's blood all over your hands. Have you been hit?"

"Yes. No." She tried to sit up. "My side hurts." She couldn't make sense of it. She probed her chest and then brought her hands up. "Everything seems okay except," she said, "my side and my hands."

"You're not okay. The guy in there isn't okay." He jerked a thumb towards the shop, "and what's this guy doing here?" He pointed at Michael.

"I was bringing Myri some tamales," Michael explained, "when this dog started barking and running crazy towards the shop."

"And what is she doing here?" Greg nodded towards LuAnn.

"My dog," LuAnn said impatiently. "Why does Zoe keep coming down here? I'm tired of chasing after her every damn night."

Michael muscled his way back into the conversation. "And then I came into the shop and the guy in there had a gun."

"Stop." Greg shoved his hands in Michael's face. "Myri, you better tell me what happened. Did you shoot Valentine?"

"I didn't shoot him. He was shooting at me," Myri said. "The bullet must have ricocheted off the walls and hit him."

"I want to believe you. He was a nasty man. I'd understand if you did shoot him."

"She didn't have a gun." Michael took off his jacket and draped it around Myri's shoulder. "I saw it all. She jumped in front of me. He fired. I can't explain it, but that's what happened. "

"A ricochet right through the head of a man who just happened to have a tackle box full of one-ounce Maple Leaf gold pieces at his feet?"

Myri gasped. "What?" Her dad always said that his old truck was worth its weight in gold.

CHAPTER TWENTY-TWO

New Visions

Days later, Myri sat in her living room with sore, bandaged hands and taped cracked ribs. What had actually happened was a mystery to everyone, Greg, Michael, herself. A bullet had grazed her side, probably knocking her to the floor, the medics suggested, causing the cracked ribs. But most of the blood had been Valentines. She didn't tell anyone of the bliss, or coming back into her body.

Now here she was, alone with a brand new key to a lockbox, a package from Michael, and Ruby's parting words. *You have work to do It's for you as well as Michael.* Myri could still feel the weight and texture of the gold as she packaged the coins, ten to a tube, twelve tubes, at current market prices, almost a $150,000.

She opened the package from Michael, a UPS box filled with plastic peanuts. Out of the protective filler came a plate wrapped in the Long Beach Weekly newspaper. The plate was divided into jade green and aqua. A little girl with red pigtails, dressed in a pink pinafore was in the lower right. She held the string to a bright yellow kite trailing blue, white and red ribbons. There was a note. *My latest creation. I've decided to stay at Way of Compassion for another six months. No tamales here but lots of good vibes. Drop by sometime. Regards, Michael.*

Only Ruby's words remained a mystery. Did Myri have more work to do, or was saving Michael the work, and now done? What did she need to do for herself? She desperately wanted to talk with someone who would understand. She found Molly Seward's card tucked behind her library card. It was time to get help from her psychic healer.

"Hi, Molly, this is Myri Wolfen. I had an appointment a few weeks back and didn't make it." She waited for a reply. "Well, I am totally confused," her voice cracked, "and you said I could talk to you on the phone." Words gushed out of her. "I think I died and then I had to come back but I didn't want to and strange things keep happening to me and now I have all this money.

What?" she paused, "Would you say that again?" Myri hit the speaker button.

"I said, 'Relax, Myri.' You aren't alone and you aren't in charge."

"Relax?"

"You might think about moving, and remember, you aren't alone. You have gifts. You can trust yourself."

Myri hung the phone up, remembering her dad's final words. Trust yourself, he'd said. You'll figure it out, he said. She picked up Michael's plate. It was bright, smooth, and beautiful. She set it on the table and pulled out the newspaper wrapping. She smoothed the wrinkled paper. Local News. She could almost smell the salty air, feel the sand between her toes, taste the briny richness of oyster. She read the weekly meals on wheels menu. The next item made her tingle. Her hands warmed, throbbed, seemed to match her heartbeat. *New Culinary Program in Clatsop Community College Begins in May.* May, her birth month. A first step to becoming a chef. Near Seaview, at the ocean. The signs were all there. No way should she pass up this chance. She would trust herself. She would go. Her life awaited her.

The End—or Perhaps a Beginning

Myri's Favorite Poems

MORNING CALLS

I hear the crows, their rough, jointed caws
cartwheel over cucumber vines,
and silky, thick-waisted eggplant,

settle on harvesting ants.
I step into the sunshine,
drag a chair to the middle of the deck,

sit with the ripening day, alert to three
quail
scratching under the green beans,
listen to a magpie and a squirrel

in the walnut tree tease a frantic
dachshund yapping below.
Scents of basil, lavender, and rose,

infuse me, swelling my heart
so large, I have no skin.
The whole world comes in.

SUMMER BOUQUET*

Just like that damn rose
to hog center stage,
its Calypso-Red skirts
flared, outward bound,
royally confident, the jewel
in a tangle of grapevines
rambling over the chain link fence
host to a glut of sparrows that flit,
squeak and holler, a gypsy band of
foragers,
an opener for the full throated lady.

The hibiscus are scandalous this year,
full of themselves, red and pink,
wanton hussies, one-day-stands,
opening wider, wider, their pistils upright,
yellow anther fully exposed
fearless in the scorching August sun.

*Published 2014 by *Everyday Poets*

MALLARD MOON

Close to the river bank,
in weedy shallows,
a shiny-green-headed
mallard flips butt up,
centered in a circle of his own
creation, offers the sky
a feather moon.

BE CAREFUL WHAT YOU WISH FOR

If the earth's crust
were a trampoline,
flappable,
the grey schnauzer might
in time,
articulate
a bounce high enough
to snag the yellow
cat, stretched sphinx-wise
on the thick-boned branch
of the apricot tree,
and return to ground
with a mouthful of fury.

Jane Roop

Jane Roop lives in Kennewick, Washington, home of the Kennewick Man, at the confluence of three rivers: the Columbia, the Snake, and the Yakima. She shares her life on an acre with two apricot trees, four apple trees, two cherry trees, three plum trees, one pear tree, one peach tree, a huge garden, spouse Joe of nearly fifty years, and one cat Bandit.

Her biggest adventures include sailing from San Francisco to Hawaii on a fifty-one foot sailboat named The Sugar Bear and living in Paris, France for nearly two years. After retiring from her business as a securities broker, she's devoting more time to her writing passions, which include fiction and poetry. She has one daughter and two grandsons. She received a BA in English from Washington State University in Pullman, Washington and an MBA from Marymount University in Arlington, VA.

Connect with Jane at JaneRoopAuthor.weebly.com and on facebook.com/jane.roop.1